Dear Reader,

This month, Silhouette Desire is celebrating milestones, miniseries—and, of course, sensual, emotional and compelling love stories. Every book is a treasured keeper in Lass Small's miniseries THE KEEPERS OF TEXAS, but this month, the continuation of this wonderful series about the Keeper family marks a milestone for Lass—the publication of her 50th book for Silhouette with *The Lone Texan*, also our MAN OF THE MONTH selection!

Desire is also proud to present the launch of two brand-new miniseries. First, let us introduce you to THE RULEBREAKERS, Leanne Banks's fabulous new series about three strong and sexy heroes. Book one is *Millionaire Dad*—and it's a story you won't want to miss. Next, meet the first of a few good men and women in uniform in the passion-filled new series BACHELOR BATTALION, by Maureen Child. The first installment, *The Littlest Marine*, will utterly delight you.

Continuing this month is the next book in Peggy Moreland's series TEXAS BRIDES about the captivating McCloud sisters, *A Sparkle in the Cowboy's Eyes*. And rounding out the month are two wonderful novels—*Miranda's Outlaw* by Katherine Garbera, and *The Texas Ranger and the Tempting Twin* by Pamela Ingrahm.

I hope you enjoy all six of Silhouette Desire's love stories this month—and every month.

Regards,

Melissa Senate

Melissa Senate
Senior Editor Silhouette Books

MAUREEN CHILD
THE LITTLEST MARINE

SILHOUETTE *Desire*®

Published by Silhouette Books

America's Publisher of Contemporary Romance

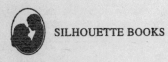

SILHOUETTE BOOKS

ISBN 0-373-76167-8

THE LITTLEST MARINE

Printed in U.S.A.

Books by Maureen Child

Silhouette Desire

Have Bride, Need Groom #1059
The Surprise Christmas Bride #1112
Maternity Bride #1138
*The Littlest Marine #1167

* Bachelor Battalion

MAUREEN CHILD

was born and raised in Southern California and is the only person she knows who longs for an occasional change of season. She is delighted to be writing for Silhouette Books, and is especially excited to be a part of the Desire line.

An avid reader, she looks forward to those rare rainy California days when she can curl up and sink into a good book. Or two. When she isn't busy writing, she and her husband of twenty-five years like to travel, leaving their two grown children in charge of the neurotic golden retriever who is the *real* head of the household. She is also an award-winning historical writer under the names Kathleen Kane and Ann Carberry.

To Amy J. Fetzer,
friend and fellow writer—thanks for walking me through
life in the corps, and for a friendship that means
a lot to me.
Also, my thanks to Sergeant Major Robert Fetzer,
USMC, for allowing me to borrow his rank—and for
answering all of the questions I pestered
Amy with. Be happy in your new home, Amy.
You'll be missed.

One

The maid of honor and the best man were barely speaking. Other than that, the rehearsal of the rehearsal dinner seemed to be a success.

Still, Elizabeth Stone thought, nowhere was it written that as maid of honor she *had* to like the best man.

"So—" her sister, Terry, leaned in close to her and whispered beneath the hum of conversation around them "—what do you think of him? Wasn't I right? Isn't he perfect for you?"

The "he" being Harding Casey, best man, career Marine and the source of the jitters rattling around in the pit of Elizabeth's stomach.

She reached for her wineglass, took a slow sip of white Zinfandel, then answered in as low pitched a voice as possible. "I'm trying *not* to think about him."

"Ooooh," the younger woman said as her eyebrows arched high on her forehead. "Sounds promising."

Frowning slightly, Elizabeth set her wineglass down
and told herself that it was useless to argue with her sister over this. For almost a year, Terry had been trying to set her up with Harding Casey, her fiancé Mike's best friend. This little gathering was as close as she had come to succeeding.

"Look," Terry said quietly, "you two are going to be together practically every day for the next week. Wouldn't it make more sense if you at least *tried* to like him?"

"Now that you bring it up," Elizabeth said, half turning in her seat to face her sister squarely. "I still don't understand why I have to spend all week with the man. *You're* the one getting married."

"Yeah...." Terry's expression went soft and dreamy, and despite the fact that Elizabeth had no real desire of her own to get married, a small sliver of envy pierced her heart. What would it be like, she wondered, to feel what Terry so obviously felt for Mike?

In the next instant, though, she remembered that she wasn't interested in finding a man. She had her own life. A successful one, thanks very much, and she was already happy. Why should she go out looking for someone who would only require her to make all kinds of changes in what she considered a darn near perfect existence?

With that thought firmly in mind, she prodded her sister. "Terry, you know I'm delighted to be your maid of honor, but—"

"No *buts,*" she interrupted. "You promised that you would help out, Lizzie."

"Sure, but why—"

"There's no way I can do all of the little things that have to be done this week." Terry leaned forward and clutched her sister's hand. "Come on, Lizzie. You can handle Harding for one little week, can't you?"

There was a challenge if ever she'd heard one. Grimly Elizabeth shot a covert glance at the man across from her. Black hair, cut into a military, "high and tight" haircut, strong jaw, straight nose, well-shaped mouth, and eyes blue enough to make Paul Newman's look a dingy gray. Standing up, he was six-feet-five inches of solid muscle, had a voice deep enough to cause earthquakes and made her stomach pitch with nerves and expectation with a single glance. Sure. She could handle him. No problem.

Lordy, she was in trouble. The only thing that kept her from having some serious fantasies about the man was the uniform he wore so proudly.

Muffling a sigh, she said softly, "Little sister, you should understand better than anyone else why I don't want anything to do with a military type."

Terry did nothing to hide her grumble of frustration. "Honestly, Lizzie, you would think you grew up manacled to a wall."

"Yeah. A wall that was reassigned every two or three years."

Elizabeth, known as "Lizzie" only to her family, had hated growing up as a Marine brat. Shifting from place to place, moving wherever their father's orders had taken them. Never really at home. Making new friends only to leave them behind. The one constant in her life...the one friend she had always been able to count on was Terry. Her sister. Who had grown up to fall in love with a Marine. But at least Terry's soon-to-be husband had left the Corps.

Harding Casey—Hard Case to his friends, looked like a lifer to her.

"You just hate the military."

"No, I don't," Elizabeth said. "I've just served my time, that's all. You've got to be relieved that Mike left the Corps. Admit it."

"I told him he didn't have to. It was his decision."

"A good one, too." Elizabeth reached for her wineglass, then rethought it and settled her hand in her lap. "At least you won't be stumping all around the world like Mom did, trying to make homes out of impersonal barracks buildings."

"Jeez, Lizzie—" Terry's voice dropped as she shot a quick look at the other diners to make sure no one could hear them "—you make it all sound so ugly. We had a great family. A terrific life. We've seen places most people only dream about."

True, Elizabeth thought. All true. But while they had been traveling around the world like modern-day gypsies, all Elizabeth had ever wanted was a home. A real home. One where she could stay put for more than three years. One where she could paint the walls any color she liked and not even consider who might be moving in after she'd gone.

Apparently, whatever gypsy gene Terry had inherited from their parents had bypassed Elizabeth altogether.

"Yeah," Elizabeth said quietly. "It was terrific."

Terry grinned, obviously not hearing the sarcasm. "Okay, now tell me how right I was about Harding. He *is* a babe, isn't he?"

Babe? Oh, he was more than a babe. But there was no way she would admit as much to Terry. She shot Harding Casey a covert glance only to find him watching her through those incredible eyes of his. Goose bumps raced up her arms. Her heartbeat quickened, and her palms were suddenly damp. This was no ordinary attraction to a handsome man. It was almost as if something inside her...*recognized* him. As if he was someone she had been waiting for.

Get a grip, she told herself as the ridiculous thought took root.

Grab her, Harding thought. Grab her, kiss her, caress her...he shook his head slightly in a vain attempt to rid himself of the almost-overpowering impulses throbbing inside him. Impulses that had been haunting him since meeting Elizabeth Stone three hours ago.

Her chin length, curly brown hair seemed to tempt him to spear his fingers through it. Those even darker brown eyes of hers mesmerized him, and he wanted to lose himself in their depths, discover her secrets. He called on years of strict military training to hide his reaction to her figure. A body made for lounging beside a fire and quiet, private picnics on moonlit beaches. His gaze slipped lower, and Harding felt something in his chest stagger. The deep vee neckline of her red silk blouse gaped a bit as she leaned in toward her sister. He caught a fleeting glimpse of pale ivory flesh and felt his mouth go dry.

He was in big trouble.

Harding shifted his gaze from Elizabeth's face to the bottle of beer in front of him. He *had* to quit staring at her. Curling his fingers around the still-cold bottle, he lifted it and took a long drink.

"So, you old Devil Dog," Mike Hall whispered as he leaned in close. "What do you think of our Lizzie?"

A brief smile touched Harding's lips, then faded. Devil Dog. The traditional greeting between Marines. Even though Mike had left the Corps a year ago, after meeting and falling in love with Terry, clearly the Corps hadn't left him.

But, *Lizzie?*

He risked another quick look at the woman opposite him, reminding himself not to eat her alive with his eyes. No, she was no *Lizzie*. Definitely an *Elizabeth*.

Perhaps, he mused, *Beth*.

"C'mon Hard Case," Mike prodded. "What's the verdict?"

He forced a casual shrug. "She seems…nice."

"Nice?" Mike looked at him, astonished. "A solid year I've been telling you about her, and all you can say when you finally meet her is that she seems *nice?*"

"Yeah, you told me about her." Harding snorted a smothered laugh. "You also told me about how she hated growing up in the Corps. And about all the grief she gave you when she was trying to get Terry to dump you."

Mike frowned. "She was trying to protect her sister."

"Sure, by taking shots at you and the Corps."

"She's changed. She likes me now." Mike shook his head slowly. "Finally figured out that I really do love Terry."

Fine. He could understand defending and protecting a sister. But Elizabeth Stone had made his friend miserable for almost six months. The fact that she was gorgeous didn't make up for that. He took a long swig of his beer. "Great, she likes you," he said slowly. "But she still hates the Corps."

Mike shrugged. "Terry says that Lizzie never liked all of the moving around their folks did while they were growing up. Even I don't think that's an easy way to raise kids…which is why I got out."

"I still can't believe you left."

"Twenty years was long enough for me."

"Not me," Harding said flatly. Why any man would give up the Corps for a woman was simply beyond him. The Marines had given him everything. A home. A family that included every Marine stationed anywhere in the world. A sense of belonging…of doing something for his country.

Nope. He would *never* give up all that to please a woman who would probably just end up leaving him, anyway.

"You and she would be great together."

Harding scowled. "Butt out, buddy."

"Hell, Hard Case." Mike sat back, shaking his head. "You're in worse shape than I thought."

He snapped his friend an irritated look.

Mike ignored it. "If you don't know a gorgeous, successful woman when you see her, the Corps ought to drum you out on the grounds of failing eyesight."

"Very funny."

"I'm serious."

"Will you let it go?"

"Probably not," Mike admitted.

"What is it with you and your kind?"

Mike laughed easily. He was still the only person Harding had ever known who was unimpressed with the patented Hard Case glare.

"What do you mean, my kind?"

Harding took another swallow of beer, deliberately kept his gaze from sliding toward Elizabeth and concentrated instead on getting his best friend off his back. "You Noah's Ark people."

Mike laughed again, but Harding went right on, warming to his theme.

"The minute you find somebody, you're just not happy until everyone around you is traveling in pairs." He kept his voice low so that only Mike would be able to hear him above the hum of other conversations taking place in the crowded, oceanfront restaurant. As he talked, he saw that Mike's smile faded. "You try every which way to drag the rest of us off, kicking and screaming toward some fairy-tale ending. Some of us are meant to be alone, you know.

Not everybody finds happily ever after. Hell, not everyone is *looking* for it.''

Leaning forward, resting his forearms on his thighs, Mike held his beer bottle cupped in both hands and stared at it thoughtfully before saying quietly, ''You need more than the Corps, Hard Case.''

He snorted. ''Look who's talking. You joined up the same time I did. For twenty years, the Corps was enough for you.''

''I retired when I found out different.''

''Yeah.'' Harding shook his head. He still couldn't understand how a man walked away from his whole life without a backward glance. As for himself, he was in the Corps for the long haul. He already had twenty years in, and he planned on staying until they threw him out. Bodily.

How did Mike stand it, going from gunnery sergeant of a batallion to head of security for some civilian computer firm?

''There *is* life off the base,'' his friend commented as if reading his mind.

''Not so I've noticed.''

''You know,'' Mike said, and this time his voice held a tinge of the old impatience, ''they should have named you Hard *Head,* instead of Hard Case.''

Harding swallowed a smile along with the last of his beer, then set the empty bottle down on the table.

''That's it for me,'' Mike said and stood up. ''I know when to quit.''

''Never have before,'' Harding pointed out.

''For tonight, Hard Case. Only for tonight.'' Mike grinned again and patted his friend's shoulder as he moved around the table. "But for right now, I think I'll steal a dance with your date. I'll even let you borrow my gorgeous, almost bride for a quick spin around the floor."

Mike took Elizabeth's hand and led her onto the shining wooden dance floor. And even when the rest of the wedding party left the table to join the dancers, Harding's gaze never left them.

Two

The recorded easy-rock music swelled softly, drowning conversation.

Harding looked at Terry and found her watching him with a knowing smile.

"Pretty, isn't she?"

Just what he needed—another prospective matchmaker. He shook his head and stood up. Walking to her side, he said, "Don't you start on me, too."

Terry was a good dancer, but short enough that Harding felt as though he was doubled over on the dance floor. He nodded as she talked, and hoped he wasn't agreeing to anything he would regret later. But dammit, he just couldn't seem to keep his mind on what she was saying. Instead, his gaze continued to dart around the floor, following Elizabeth and Mike's progress. She smiled at his friend, and Harding's insides tightened.

One song led into the next and he hardly noticed, until Mike and Elizabeth stopped alongside them.

"Okay, pal," Mike said. "You've had enough time with that gorgeous woman, and this one—" he jerked his head to indicate Elizabeth "—keeps begging me to get you to dance with her."

"Mike!"

Her future brother-in-law ignored her as he deftly pulled Terry into his arms and gently shoved Elizabeth at Harding. "Have fun!" he said as they danced away.

Someone bumped into her, nudging her closer to Harding.

"Nice music," she commented, and glanced around the floor at the dancing couples.

"Yes, ma'am," he said.

She winced and tilted her head back to meet his gaze. "If we're going to be together all week, Mr. Casey, I think you should know, I *hate* being called 'ma'am.'"

"Yes, ma'am," he said deliberately. "Probably as much as I hate being called, 'Mr. Casey.'"

"What should I call you," she asked, "Sergeant?"

"It's Sergeant Major, actually."

"I know."

"That's right," he said with a short nod. "Your father is a Marine."

"Was," she corrected, loudly enough to be heard over the music. "He's retired."

"Impossible," he retorted. "Once a Marine, always a Marine."

"Yeah," she admitted on a sigh. "I know."

He decided to ignore her obvious dislike for the military. "How about you call me Harding, and I'll call you Elizabeth?"

She pulled in a long, slow, deep breath, and he fought to keep his gaze from dropping to the swell of her breasts.

"Deal," she said. "'Harding.' It's an unusual name."

He shrugged. "Old English. It means 'son of the warrior.'"

She nodded. "Naturally."

An exuberant dancer bumped against her, sending her crashing into Harding's chest. She put her hands up to stop her fall, then backed away from him quickly, as if burned.

Silence again. Two people, standing in the middle of the dance floor, surrounded by whirling couples. Stupid for the two of them to simply stand there and get trampled.

He didn't have the slightest doubt that Mike and Terry were covertly watching...hoping for *something* to happen between the two of them. In fact, that was the main reason he hadn't already asked Elizabeth to dance. He knew it was just what his old pal wanted—no, expected. Mike probably figured at the same time, though, that Harding would refuse to dance just to spite him.

With that thought firmly in mind, Harding smiled

to himself. He had always believed in keeping the enemy guessing.

"Would you like to dance?" They both said at the same time.

Harding looked at her, catching the amusement twinkling in her eyes, and found himself smiling in acknowledgment.

"There's no reason we shouldn't enjoy ourselves, is there?" Elizabeth asked.

"Not a single one," he agreed, and extended one hand toward her. As her palm brushed across his, that same sense of electricity shot up the length of his arm. He gritted his teeth and muttered, "Ooo-rah!"

"Oh, Lord," she groaned quietly.

He pulled her into his arms.

It felt as though she had been made just for him. Her head nestled beneath his chin, her breasts pressed to his chest, her hand resting lightly in his. Harding closed his eyes briefly and prayed for strength.

He felt solid, Elizabeth told herself. Right. Her left hand stole across his shoulder to the back of his neck. Miles of muscles, she thought, and briefly entertained the notion of seeing those muscles in their bare naked glory. Her breath caught in her throat, and her stomach did a series of somersaults. She stumbled slightly, then stepped quickly to get back into the rhythm of the dance.

Nope, she told herself firmly. She would *not* let him get to her. She had spent a whole year avoiding this man and, darn it, she wasn't about to cave in to hormones in one night.

Elizabeth's three-inch heels wobbled beneath her,

and Harding's arm around her waist tightened in response. Glancing up at him, she met his smile with one of her own.

"Did I step on your toes?" he asked.

Good-looking, great body *and* polite, she thought. He knew very well he hadn't stepped on her toes. He was simply covering for her misstep.

"No," she said. "My mind must have drifted." Now that had to be the biggest understatement since Custer said, "I think I see an Indian." Of course, nowadays, it would be "Native American."

"It's been a while since I've been dancing," he said.

"Me, too." Brilliant, she thought. Nothing better than some scintillating after-dinner conversation.

"So," she said, trying to say *something* intelligent, "how long have you and Mike known each other?" She already knew the answer to that one. Hadn't she been hearing Mike sing this man's praises for the past year?

"We met in boot camp."

"Long time ago?"

"Twenty years."

Oh my, yes, this conversation was getting better and better.

He executed a smooth turn that lifted the hem of her skirt to swirl around her legs. "So what made you stay in the Marines?" she asked, needing to talk to keep her mind off other, more distracting thoughts.

"What made you decide to be a cook?"

She bristled slightly. "Chef," she said. "Pastry chef, to be specific."

His eyebrows lifted. "I stand corrected." He held her tightly to him, did a series of turns that left her breathless, then led her back into a standard waltz.

When she could speak again, she tilted her head back to look into those blue eyes of his. "I enjoy cooking. I'm good at it."

"Ditto."

"Huh?"

"I enjoy being a Marine," he explained further. "I'm good at it."

"Oh." Yep, she thought. Her father would *love* this guy. Two men cut from the same cloth, so to speak. "Where are you stationed?" she asked next.

"Camp Pendleton."

She bit her tongue to stop herself from admitting that she had already known that, too. Terry and Mike talked about him all the time. She would even be willing to bet that she knew what he had for breakfast every morning. The bridal couple had not been exactly subtle in their matchmaking efforts.

"Isn't that sort of a long drive from here?"

"With traffic, about an hour."

She nodded as his thighs moved against hers. Her brain slipped into neutral. They moved through the dancing couples with an almost magical ease. Gliding, swaying around the floor, it was as if they had been dancing together for years.

The song ended, giving way to another, and they went on, oblivious to anyone else in the room.

His legs brushed hers. He threaded his thick, callused fingers through hers, and their palms met. His hand on her waist dipped a bit, coming to rest on the curve of her behind. Everywhere he touched her, Elizabeth felt as though she was on fire.

Raw, primitive heat coursed through her body, making her heart pound and her blood race. Her breasts rubbed against his chest and her nipples tightened expectantly. A damp ache settled in her center, making her thighs tremble.

How was she supposed to ignore him if her own body was working against her?

"So," he asked suddenly, "what made you change your mind about Mike and Terry?"

She squeezed her eyes shut briefly before looking up at him. "They told you I was against their marriage?"

"Yes, ma'am."

"I was afraid of that."

"Don't worry about it," Harding told her. "Mike admired you for it even while he was complaining to me about you trying to split them up."

"He did?"

"Yeah. Said you were just trying to protect your sister." His gaze settled on her. "Loyalty's something we admire in the Corps."

She nodded, understanding completely. "*Semper fi,*" she whispered.

"You got it."

Elizabeth was a little ashamed now of the hard time she had given Mike when he and Terry had started dating. And she had to give her sister's fiancé points. He hadn't given up and he hadn't held her opposition against her. "He's a nice man."

"The best." His tone changed when he added,

"I'm not so nice. You made Mike pretty miserable for a long time."

"I guess I'm not so nice, either." She stiffened in his arms. It was one thing for her to regret her own behavior privately, but she wasn't about to stand still for a lecture. "Terry's always been too romantic for her own good. I had to look out for her."

After a long moment he nodded, then asked, "And who looks out for you?"

Her stomach flip-flopped as she stared into his eyes. Ignoring it, she answered, "I do."

As another song ended, he looked down at her, his gaze clashing with hers in a silent tumult of emotion. Elizabeth drew one long, shuddering breath. What was it about this man? She wasn't a stranger to men in uniform, so that old cliché didn't hold true. Clearly then, it was something about Harding Casey himself that was getting to her. She wasn't willing to risk that. Desperately unsettled, she whispered, "I think I'd better get back home."

"Already?" That voice of his rumbled along her spine and sent every one of her nerve endings into overdrive.

Deliberately she took a step back, pulling her hand from his grasp. "Yeah. Terry wants me to run a couple of errands for her in the morning, and who knows what she and Mike will have planned for us later in the day."

"They are trying to keep us together, aren't they?"

"Terry's always been stubborn."

"Mike, too."

She nodded, telling herself to move. Get away.

Walk fast, no, *run* to a car. Any car that promised her a ride home. Why hadn't she driven herself?

Because she had listened to Terry, that's why.

"Anyway," she said, starting off the dance floor toward their table. "Thanks for the dances, and I guess I'll see you tomorrow."

"Just a minute," he said, and she glanced back to see him wind his way through the swaying couples to speak with Mike. In moments he was back again. Taking her elbow, he said, "All right, let's go."

"*Let's?* You're leaving, too?"

He shot her a quick look. "I'm taking you home."

"Oh, that's not necessary," she babbled. "I'll just grab a cab."

"Look," he said, "you came with Terry. You need a ride. I'm available. Why wait for a cab when you're ready to leave now?"

Terrific, she thought. Not just a Marine. The Sir Galahad of Marines.

"Really, Harding," she started to say.

The sentence trailed off into silence as soon as she met his gaze. There was no way this man was going to put her in a cab.

Inhaling deeply, she blew the air out in a rush and accepted the inevitable. "Okay then, let's go."

Windows down, the cold, sea-kissed air rushed in at them as Harding steered his late-model Mustang north, up Pacific Coast Highway.

"Nice car," she said after several moments of tense silence.

"Rented," he muttered.

"Where's yours?" Elizabeth asked, more out of politeness than actual curiosity.

"Don't have one."

Conversation would be a lot simpler, she told herself, if she didn't have to practically use a bayonet to force him to contribute. He'd been a heck of a lot chattier on the dance floor, she thought. Why the change? Was it because now it was just the two of them? Well, whatever the reason, Elizabeth wasn't going to sit in stony silence the whole way home.

"You live in Huntington Beach, California and don't own a car?" she asked.

He shot her a sidelong glance. "Too much trouble to own one when you're never in one place more than a few years. All that hassle with changing license plates and registration..."

A veritable *flood* of information. And with it, memories. Her father, too, had never owned a car until he and Elizabeth's mother had retired to Florida several years before.

Harding lapsed into silence again, and she bit her tongue to keep from being the one to speak first this time. But maybe she shouldn't be so hard on him, she thought. She had seen the look on his face while they danced. She knew that he had been feeling the same overpowering attraction that she had experienced. All things considered, she thought, they were doing well indeed, having *any* sort of conversation.

Although, she told herself as miles of beach road disappeared behind them, perhaps it would be better all the way around if they each simply owned up to the truth of what was happening between them. She looked at his stoic profile and knew that if they were going to get this out into the open, it would be up to her to start the ball rolling.

Before she could change her mind, she said, "This won't work, you know."

His breath left him in a rush. He gave her a brief, half smile before turning his gaze back to the road. "I'm glad you see that, too."

"Of course I do," Elizabeth told him.

Shaking his head, he went on as if she hadn't spoken. "The last thing I need in my life is a woman."

"I feel the same way," she tossed in and was rewarded with a quizzical look. Correcting herself, she said quickly, "About a man, I mean. Particularly, a Marine."

He frowned at the distinction, then nodded and started talking again, as if her words had broken a dam that had stood as long as it was able. "I tried marriage once, you know."

"No, I didn't." Strange, that with all the information Terry had given her about Harding Casey, the woman had never added the fairly pertinent point concerning a wife.

"Yeah," he said, almost to himself. "Only lasted a few months."

"What happened?"

He shrugged those massive shoulders. "She left me. Better in the end, I suppose. She couldn't handle being a Marine wife."

Unwillingly, she felt a stab of empathy for the woman. She remembered all too clearly how hard her mother had worked, trying to give her children a sense of permanence even while traipsing around the world. "It's not an easy job," she said.

He grinned, and her stomach flipped. She sincerely hoped he wouldn't do that often, during the next week they were to spend together.

"That's right. You *would* know. Your father is career Marine."

"Yeah, and you could say my mother was, too. Lord knows she should have gotten a medal or two."

He bowed his head slightly in acknowledgment. "It takes a special woman to handle it. My ex didn't like the idea of long absences, for one thing."

"Ah, deployment," she said softly, remembering all of the times her father had been gone in her life.

"Six months every eighteen months," he said.

Christmases, she thought. Summers, school plays...

"And," he went on, oblivious to her silence, "she wasn't real keen on the notion of packing up and moving every three years or so, never quite sure which base she'd end up on."

It was a hassle, she remembered, though her mother had always looked on it as another adventure. Terry, too, for that matter. Just because she herself didn't care for the life didn't mean that there weren't plenty of women who did. To be completely honest, her own mother had thrived on it.

Finally she said slowly, "You know, Harding, any woman who really loves a man can put up with just about anything. I think you just picked a lemon in the garden of love."

He came to a stop at a traffic signal and swiveled

his head to look at her in the reflected yellow glow of a fog lamp streetlight.

"You're probably right," he conceded. "But either way, once was enough for me. I won't try it again. A mistake like that is hard to correct and almost impossible to forget."

The light turned green, and he stepped on the gas.

"I agree completely." Elizabeth settled back into her seat, more comfortable than she had been all night. What a relief it was to get this all into the open. "That's why I have no intention of marrying. *Especially* a military man. Growing up with one was enough. Besides, I've yet to meet any man I would be interested in enough to even *think* about marriage." She turned her head to watch the black waves roll in toward shore. "And I like having my time to myself. I need it. To think. To work."

"I know just what you mean," he said. As they neared the Huntington Beach pier, he pulled the car close to the curb, threw it into Park and shut off the engine.

She looked at him. "What are you up to?"

"Not a thing, ma'am. Just thought you might like to take a little stroll on the beach before heading back to your place."

Odd, that once they had started talking openly about how neither of them was interested in the other, they were getting along great.

"You know something?" she said. "That sounds like a wonderful idea."

He got out, came around to her side and opened the door for her. Once he'd helped her out of the low-slung car, he released her hand and walked beside her as they crossed the street to the steps leading down to the sand.

"I'm really glad we had that little talk, Harding."

"I am, too, Elizabeth," he said. "We'll be spending a lot of time together this coming week, and there's no reason why we can't relax and enjoy each other's company. As friends."

Friends. Sure. Why not? They could do it. They were both grown-ups. Uncontrollable lust was for teenagers or for those who had no self-control.

"Friends," she agreed firmly. At the bottom of the steps, she paused to step out of her high heels.

"You should maybe keep those on at least until we're clear of the pier. There's probably broken glass all over the place."

She looked up at him briefly. "High heels and sand do not mix, Harding."

He nodded slowly, then before she could say another word, he bent down, scooped her up in his arms and cradled her against his chest.

Her heartbeat thundered in her ears. Her breathing shortened, became more difficult.

"What are you doing?" she managed to ask.

Grinning at her, he said, "Helping a *friend*."

"Oh." She swallowed with difficulty and ordered her pulse rate to slow down. "Okay."

Friend, she thought silently. Repeatedly. Maybe if she said it often enough, her body would start to believe it.

Three

Harding set his new "friend" down gently and took a step back from her. His body was on full alert. Hard. Ready. Eager. Too much more of this "friendship" and he would be a dead man.

Or maybe a live-and-in-pain one who wished he were dead.

But what was he thinking? He was a Marine. He had been in battle. Survived whizzing bullets and stupid recruits. Surely he could last out a week in the company of Elizabeth Stone.

He shot her a look from the corner of his eye and had to admit that a week with Elizabeth Stone was going to be much tougher on him than any enemy soldier with a puny little machine gun could be.

In silence they started walking along the shoreline. The tide was out, and the slow ripples of water surged sluggishly toward the beach, occasionally sneaking up close enough to them that the two people did a quick step to one side to stay dry.

Sea-air-scented wind ruffled across the surface of the ocean, and a full moon lent a silvery, almost bright, light to the darkness.

"What was Mike saying to you at the restaurant earlier?"

"Hmm?" He looked at her, thought for a minute, then said, "Oh."

"You don't have to say," she said with a gentle laugh. "I'll bet I could guess."

"Yes, you probably could." Chances were very good that Terry had been saying approximately the same things to her.

"Why do you suppose they're trying so hard to bring us together?"

He shrugged again. "They mean well."

"So did the Crusaders."

Harding laughed aloud at her gloomy tone as much as at her words.

She looked up at him and grinned. "I guess there really isn't anything we can do to stop them, is there?"

"Short of getting married?" he asked. "No."

"Well, as much as I love Terry," Elizabeth said, and bent down to pick up a piece of driftwood, "I'm not willing to marry somebody just to make her happy."

"Amen."

She tossed the stick into the receding tide and stared at it for several long moments as it rocked on the rippling surface before being pulled back out to sea. "I haven't been down here in far too long," she said wistfully.

Smiling, he echoed her earlier astonishment that he hadn't owned a car. "What? You live in California and don't go to the beach?"

She caught on to what he was doing and said, "Touché."

They started strolling again in a companionable silence. An older couple, walking a tiny dog on a long leash, passed them with a muttered greeting. From far off down the beach they saw the wavering, indistinct glow of small fires burning in the cement fire rings. On the clear, still air, laughter and snatches of campfire songs drifted to them.

But Harding paid no attention to any of it. Instead, his concentration was focused on the woman walking alongside him, carrying her high heels in one hand. He watched the soft breeze lift her dark brown curls off her neck and thought he caught the scent of her perfume. Something light and feminine and alluring, it sent daggers of need digging into his guts.

Damn, what if he had listened to Mike a year ago when his friend had first suggested he meet Elizabeth Stone? What might his life have been like these past twelve months? Torture? Or bliss?

Torture, most definitely.

Because no matter how much he wanted her...no matter how powerful the attraction was between them...he wouldn't allow anything to come of it.

In fact, he couldn't imagine why Mike and Terry had thought to pair the two of them up, anyway. They couldn't be more different. He snorted a choked laugh and shook his head.

"What's so funny?" she asked. Reaching up, she plucked at a long strand of windblown hair that had attached itself to her eyelashes.

"Just thinking," he answered. "Mike and Terry must have been nuts to believe you and I—"

"Nuts," she agreed.

"Me, a career Marine, and—" he stopped, cocked his head at her and wondered aloud "—what is it you're called? The Princess of Party Cooking?"

Now Elizabeth laughed. "Some reviewer gave me that tag a couple of years ago." She shrugged. "My publisher loved it and ran with it. The name stuck. But all I really am is a pastry chef."

"Who writes bestselling cookbooks."

"*Co*writes," she countered, holding up one finger to admonish him. "Which means, I supply the recipes and a few humorous stories about some of my more memorable disasters and Vicki, the writer I work with, puts it all together and makes me sound brilliant."

Harding looked at her, surprise gleaming in his eyes. "Not many people would admit that they don't actually write their own books."

She smiled at him. "No point in denying it. Vicki's name is right there on the cover."

"And whose idea was that?"

Elizabeth's gaze shifted to the darkness of the sea. "Mine," she admitted. "I can cook, but I can't write, and I don't want to take bows for something I didn't do."

He knew lots of people who wouldn't have been bothered by that in the least. There was more to Elizabeth Stone than just the way she kicked his hormones into high gear.

Moving away from those ideas, he instead focused on what he had been thinking before. "Still, what could a Marine and a 'princess' possibly have in common?"

"Not much, besides knowing two people with way too much time on their hands."

"True."

She swiveled her head to look at him, and one glance from those dark, fathomless eyes of hers and he felt as keyed up and tightly strung as he did the night before a battle.

He sucked in a quick, deep breath and saw her do the same before she turned away abruptly.

Elizabeth bent down, picked up another, longer stick and turned her back on the ocean.

"What are you doing?" he asked, silently grateful that she had broken eye contact.

"Something I haven't done in years," she said, and started writing her name in the water-soaked sand at the edge of the tide.

He stood to one side and watched her.

When she had finished with her own name, she went on, inscribing his name, using the last *H* in Elizabeth as the first *H* in Harding. Her task complete, she tossed the stick aside and stood back, admiring her handiwork. Then she looked up at him expectantly.

"Very nice," he said. "Until the tide shifts." Then

the ocean would run in, obliterating their names like an eraser moving over a chalkboard.

"Nothing is forever," she told him, and as she spoke a rogue surge of water rushed across her ankles and sluiced past her feet. The seawater rippled across their names in a haphazard pattern, and in a moment most of the script was gone.

"See?" she said with a lightness that didn't quite cover the note of disappointment in her voice. Then, glancing down at her soaking wet nylons, she grimaced and walked away from the ocean's edge, closer to him. "Hold these for a minute, will you?" she asked, and handed him her heels.

As she lifted the hem of her already short skirt, he tensed and asked, "What are you doing?"

Bent at the waist, she looked up at him briefly. "I'm just going to take off these nylons."

"Out here?" Did his voice sound as strained to her as it did to him?

"There's nobody around but you and me."

That only made things worse.

Harding took in another deep gulp of cold air and hoped it would do something to stop the flames erupting inside him. As a gentleman should, he half turned, to give her some privacy. Besides, there was no point in torturing himself.

She saw the movement and chuckled. "Don't worry about it, Harding. They're not panty hose."

Oh, God, he thought, closing his eyes on a quiet groan. *Garters?*

"They're just thigh-highs," she went on, when he still didn't turn back toward her.

Thigh-highs. *Black* thigh-highs. His body tightened at the mental image of lace and sheer black fabric hugging and caressing those long legs of hers.

"For heaven's sake, Harding," she said. "Look at me. You would see more flesh if I was wearing shorts!"

He turned around, then, and bit back another, deeper groan. It was worse than he had thought. Thigh-highs indeed. Apparently Elizabeth Stone was completely unaware of just how seductive she looked.

The wide, black lace elastic band hugged the creamy white flesh of her upper thigh and gave way to sheer, black silk covering the rest of her leg. Slowly she smoothed her palms along the stocking, rolling the fragile material beneath her fingertips, exposing her pale white skin, inch by tantalizing inch.

Mouth dry, throat tight, he watched her, unable and unwilling to look away. Her hands moved down her leg, and his palms itched to help her.

By the time she had removed the first stocking, his breathing was strangled. When she started in on the second, bending over slowly to complete the task, his gaze shifted to the curve of her behind beneath the short, tight black skirt.

His fingers tightened around the shoes he held in one hand until he felt the tips of the high heels dig into his palm. He deliberately concentrated on that small discomfort in order to take his mind off the nearly overwhelming pain of his aching groin.

Finally she straightened up and tossed her hair back out of her eyes. "That feels better," she said, balling her wet nylons up in her hands. "Nothing worse than soggy stockings."

"Uh-huh." He could think of a few things worse.

"Harding?"

He swallowed heavily. "Yes, ma'am?"

"You okay?"

"Yeah," he ground out. "I'm fine." Or he would be as soon as he could get back to the base and stand under a cold shower for two or three hours. Or days.

"You don't *look* fine."

"Forget it."

She blinked, surprised at his gruff tone. "Okay."

"Look," he said, more hotly than he had planned, "we talked about this. How whatever it was we're feeling for each other won't work."

"So?"

"So, I'd appreciate you not making this any harder than it already is."

"I made it harder by taking off my stockings?"

Rock hard, he thought.

"Jeez, Harding, relax." She shook her head and turned her face into the wind. "We're both adults. We can handle this...attraction without acting on it."

"I didn't say I was going to act on it. I *said* you were making things more difficult than they had to be."

"Aren't you overreacting just a little?"

"I don't think so."

"Maybe," she said with a long look at his obviously uncomfortable expression, "you'd better take me back home, then."

Now *that* sounded like a plan. Get out from under

the damn full moon, away from the soft, sea-scented breezes and the lulling, hypnotic rush of the ocean. Once distanced from this romantic setting, it would be easier to stick to the friendship they had so recently agreed upon.

"That's probably a good idea," he said abruptly.

"I'll take those," she muttered, and reached for her shoes.

She moved in close, destroying his good intentions. Her scent surrounded him. Her warmth called to him, and he couldn't withstand it. His resolve disappeared. Instead of giving her the shoes, he dropped them to the sand and grabbed her hand. Harding felt it again immediately. That sudden jolt of awareness. Of heat. Electricity. And she felt it, too. He could see it in her eyes.

Instinctively he pulled her closer. Without a word she moved into the circle of his arms and tilted her head back for his kiss. Moonlight dusted her features, and even as he bent to claim her mouth, he knew he shouldn't. Knew that once the line was crossed it would be impossible to go back.

The wind picked up, and the roar of the ocean sounded all around them.

He brushed his lips across hers gently, once. Twice. Then his mouth came down on hers with a hard, steady pressure, and a crashing wave of sensation fell on him. As if the night sky were lit up with fireworks, he felt himself come to life. He felt an intense connection with this woman, and when she suddenly broke away and took a staggering step back from him, it was as if he'd been dunked in a pool of ice water.

Breathless and stunned at her reaction to a simple kiss, Elizabeth took a step away from the man who had just touched her so deeply. It was small consolation to see her own shocked feelings etched into the Marine's stoic features.

"All right," she whispered, and started walking backward, keeping a wary eye on him. "Maybe you weren't overreacting." She shook her head and added, "We can't do this, Harding. *I* can't do this." Then she turned and ran across the sand. She raced toward the pier and the street beyond where there were lights, people and a car that could carry her back to her house.

To safety.

She heard him running after her and knew that she would never be able to beat him. He had years of training behind him while all she had to show for exercise was a folded-up treadmill that made an excellent silent butler.

Before she got close to the steps leading back to the street, Harding caught up with her. Grabbing her upper arm, he turned her around to face him.

"Why did you run?"

Why was he pretending he didn't know the answer to that?

"You know why."

He reached up and ran one hand across his severe military haircut. "You don't have to run from me," he growled. "I wouldn't hurt you."

"I know that," she snapped, irritated with herself more than him. Good Lord, she was thirty-two years old. She had been kissed before. Often. Why was she reacting like a giddy teenager on her first date?

Because, a voice in the back of her mind answered, she had never been kissed like *that* before.

"Look, Harding," she said, trying to explain something that just might prove to be unexplainable. "I wasn't scared. Exactly. Just…surprised." Stunned would have been a better word. "I guess I wasn't really running away from you—it was more like running from whatever it is that happens between us whenever we get too close."

He nodded abruptly, his mouth thinning into a grim line. "I know the feeling."

"You were right when you said we shouldn't make this more difficult than it already is." Elizabeth forced a deep breath of cold air into her lungs. "Why start something that neither one of us has any intention of finishing?"

He looked at her for a long, slow minute. "The only reason I can think of, is that Marines don't run."

She choked out a laugh. "I'm not a Marine."

"No," he said and pulled her close to him. "But I am."

This time, when their lips met, Elizabeth was prepared for the incredible sensations skittering inside her. At least she thought she was. She gasped as the opening ripples of excitement coursed through her, then she gave herself up to the inevitable. She had known from the moment she had first looked into his blue eyes that this kiss was coming, and instead of worrying about the repercussions, gave herself up to the wonder of it.

He parted her lips with the tip of his tongue, and when she opened for him, he plundered her mouth like an invading army. Daggers of desire pricked at her insides, and when he held her tighter, closer, she pressed herself into him, flattening her breasts against his chest.

He cupped the back of her head, his fingers combing through her hair and she reached up, wrapped her arms around his neck and held on as if afraid she was about to slip off the edge of the world. His right hand moved across her back, down her spine to the curve of her bottom. He followed that curve and held her against his hardness. An answering need blossomed inside her, and she moaned gently.

Tearing his mouth from hers, Harding dipped his head to lavish damp kisses along the length of her neck. His arms tightened around her like twin bands of twisted steel. Desire screamed inside her. The feeling was more, so much more than she had expected. Elizabeth had the wild, insane desire to rip off her clothes and offer herself to him there. In the sand.

She craved his touch more than her next breath.

"Harding," she whispered, "I want—"

"Way to go, soldier boy!" A loud voice, filled with laughter, splintered the moment.

Harding straightened abruptly, pulled her close to him protectively and shielded her while she pulled herself together.

Laughter floated down to them from the pier above, and after a moment or two, shuffling footsteps told them that their audience had moved on.

She buried her face against Harding's chest.

"Damn teenagers," he muttered. "They're everywhere. What I wouldn't give to get that kid in boot camp."

"Good God," Elizabeth groaned, her voice muffled. "What were we doing…thinking?"

"Thinking didn't have much to do with what we were doing," he told her and stood stock-still for a long moment, keeping his arms firmly around her. Finally though, he said, "C'mon. I'll take you back to your place."

Elizabeth drew in a long, shuddering breath as he lifted her into his arms again to carry her across the glass-littered sand. Ridiculous, but she almost enjoyed being carried around like some modern-day Jane to his Tarzan. She had never known a man strong enough to lift her not-so-small form as easily as he would have a child.

Her arm around his shoulders, she tried not to think about the hard, corded muscles lying just beneath his uniform. Or about how much she would love to feel his naked strength beneath her fingertips.

When she thought she could speak without her voice shaking, she tried to lighten the incredibly tension-filled moment. "I thought you said Marines don't run?"

He glanced at her, then shifted his gaze to a point above her head. "They don't. But they have been known to make a strategic retreat now and again…when absolutely necessary."

"Like now?"

"Princess, *exactly* like now."

Four

"Look, Harding," she said and stared up into those lake blue eyes of his. "I don't think this friendship thing is going to work."

"Probably not," he conceded as he set her down on the sidewalk.

Surprised, she nodded at him thoughtfully and pushed the button for the Walk signal. "Somehow, I had the feeling you were going to prove to be one of those die-hard Marines."

"Meaning what, exactly?" The light changed. He took her elbow and guided her across Pacific Coast Highway.

"Meaning," she said, forcing herself to keep up with his much-longer stride, "not knowing when to give up. Surrender."

He stopped alongside the car and looked down at

her. One corner of his mouth quirked, and her insides jumped. Ignoring the sudden rush of adrenaline to the pit of her stomach, Elizabeth went on. "I mean, since we both know that friendship has already been blown out of the water, we can simply call Mike and Terry and tell them that the deal's off. We can each help out…we're just not going to be doing it together."

"Nope."

It took a moment for that one word to sink in.

"What do you mean, 'nope'?"

"I mean," he said, opening the car door for her, "I have no intention of telling Mike that I can't handle being around you for a week."

"But—"

"Princess," he said, "I've been in battle. I've been stranded in jungles with nothing to eat but my own shoes." His voice deepened as he loomed over her, and Elizabeth's head fell back on her neck as she struggled to maintain eye contact. "I've taken lazy, unmotivated teenagers and made them into first-class Marines. I've been in charge of *hundreds* of men and tons of equipment."

"So?" she managed to ask.

"So, I'm damn sure *not* running up the white flag because of a couple of kisses." That said, he jerked his head toward the car. "Now, get in and I'll take you home."

Bristling at the command, Elizabeth pitched her wet shoes and stockings into the car, planted her fists on her hips and gave him a glare guaranteed to melt stone. "We're not leaving yet, Marine."

His black eyebrows lifted.

Who the hell did he think he was? Did he really think that *he* could ignore her better than *she* could ignore him? This was precisely why she had always steered clear of the military type. Giving orders was second nature to them. Well, if he thought he could tell *her* to do *anything,* he had a big surprise coming.

Poking him in the chest with the tip of her index finger, she went on. "I've never been in battle or a jungle. But I have faced down a hungry crowd with nothing to feed them but a ruined soufflé and over-done bread. I've met deadlines, done book tours that left me so tired, death looked like a vacation, and, mister, there isn't a Marine *alive* who can outlast *me.*"

He opened his mouth to speak, but she cut him off.

"And as for those kisses, don't flatter yourself. I've been kissed before, buster—and if that's the best you've got, believe me, I'll be able to keep from hurling myself at your manly chest."

A glimmer of a smile raced across his features, then disappeared.

"Manly chest, eh?"

"A figure of speech," she said. A *true* figure of speech, but that was beside the point. Also beside the point was the fact that she had lied about the potency of his kisses. Sure she had been kissed before. But never like that.

"You finished?" he asked.

"For now."

He nodded slowly. "Fine, I just want to say one thing."

"What?"

"You may be tougher than you look, princess. But *this* Marine can outlast *you* anytime."

"Humph!" She'd lost track of exactly what they were talking about here, so she figured that answer was her only safe one.

"Then we're agreed?" he asked.

"Agreed," she snapped, then added, "Agreed on what?"

"That a couple of kisses are no reason to admit defeat."

"Oh. Sure."

"Fine, then, it's settled." He set one hand on the top of the car door and ushered her inside with the other. "We can't be friends, but we can last out the week in each other's company."

"No problem," she said firmly, and settled back in the seat as he closed the car door and walked around to the other side. He slid into the driver's seat, jammed the key into the ignition, then looked at her before firing up the engine.

Blue eyes locked with brown. Elizabeth's heartbeat jumped into high gear. The palms of her hands were sweaty, and deep within her a core of heat burst into flame.

"No problem," she whispered.

"Right," he said, with as little conviction as she felt.

The South Coast Plaza mall was packed. Saturday-morning crowds teemed through the cavernous place. Moms pushing strollers, crying babies, lounging teenagers, professional types with cell phones glued to their ears all competed for walking room.

Elizabeth came to an abrupt stop beside the escalator. A stroller clipped her heel and rolled on past without even slowing down. She winced, shot the oblivious mother a glare, then turned back to the man on her right.

Harding looked hopelessly out of place. That spit-and-polish Marine exterior stood out like several sore thumbs, in the midst of suburbia. She shook her head as she looked up—*way* up at him. Without the benefit of her three-inch heels, Elizabeth felt short for the first time in her life.

Mercy, he was gorgeous. Just for a moment she allowed herself to remember how it had felt to be cradled against that massive chest of his. Memories rushed into her brain. The strength of his arms. The warmth of his kiss.

The abrupt way he'd left her at her front door the night before.

She drew one deep, shaky breath. This was going to be a long week.

"So what's first?" Harding asked, startling Elizabeth out of her reverie.

"Oh!" She glanced down at the list in her hand. Her sister, Terry, was nothing if not efficient. On the small memo pad, there was a different list for every day during this last hectic week before the wedding. Looking under Saturday, Elizabeth read out loud, "Pick up going-away dress at the Flim Flam."

"Flim Flam?" Harding echoed.

"A new dress shop here in the mall."

He nodded. "Anything else?"

"Yeah, she wants us to pick up Mike's wedding present at Macy's."

"Where's that?" Harding asked, staring into the distance.

"At the other end of the mall." Elizabeth checked her watch. They had plenty of time, actually, but it gave her something to do. "Why don't you go to Macy's, I'll pick up her dress then meet you at the coffee bar."

"All right," he said. "What am I picking up?"

She laughed shortly. "Sorry. Go to the jewelry counter. Terry bought him a watch last week, and the engraving is finally done. They'll be holding it for her there." She dug into her shoulder bag and came up with a receipt. Handing it to him, she said, "Show them this. You shouldn't have a problem. It's already paid for."

He glanced at the paper, folded it neatly into fours, then tucked it into his pants pocket.

"Macy's is right at the end of that concourse," she told him, pointing off to the left.

He smirked at her. "I think I'll be able to find it."

She shrugged. "Okay then, see you at the coffee bar in one hour."

Elizabeth turned to go, but he grabbed her hand, pulling her back to his side. Carefully he checked the time on her wristwatch, then adjusted hers to match his exactly.

"Synchronizing our watches?" she said on a muffled laugh.

"Yep." He gave her a brief nod, then said, "Coffee bar, eleven hundred thirty hours."

She stifled the groan building in her chest. Memories of all the years she had spent living according to military time flashed through her brain and left again just as quickly. It didn't matter. She was through with all of that. She and Harding were only going to be around each other for a week—there was no point in arguing with him all the time.

"Fine. Eleven-thirty. The coffee bar's on the second level," she said, "right next to—"

"I'll find it."

"But this mall is really big, Harding. It can be very confusing." Elizabeth shopped there all the time, and even she had been known to lose her bearings a time or two.

He gave her a slow, patronizing, infuriating smile as he shook his head. "Elizabeth, in the Corps, I am what is known as a pathfinder."

That was a new one to her. One eyebrow rose as she asked, "As in *Last of the Mohicans?*"

He frowned briefly. "As in I am trained to be able to survive in a jungle with nothing but a piece of string and a knife. I *think* I'll be able to find my way around a shopping center."

She felt she should point out that very few jungles are equipped with banks of elevators, hundreds of people, strolling musicians, a double-decker carousel and dozens of corridors, each of them just like the last. But…who was she to argue with a pathfinder?

"Okay, Hawkeye," Elizabeth said with a half smile. "Go to it! On my mark, I'll meet you in one hour.'' She looked down at her watch, snapped out "Mark!" then turned on her heel and disappeared into the crowds.

Amazing. One minute she was there and the next she wasn't. In the constantly shifting crowd of people, he couldn't even catch a glimpse of her. He didn't even want to *think* about what this place must be like during the Christmas shopping rush.

Minutes ticked by before he told himself to get moving. He wanted to be sitting at that blasted coffee bar having a nice, leisurely snack by the time she arrived. Mumbling "Excuse me" to the elderly woman who crashed right into him, Harding stepped onto the escalator and descended into Suburban Hell.

Fifty-five minutes later, Harding tightened his grip on the small Macy's package in his hand and started down yet another corridor. He glanced from storefront to storefront, sure he'd been that way before. Frowning, he came to a dead stop in front of a kitchenware shop. Dammit, he recognized that three-foot-tall chicken in the display window. Either he was walking in circles or there was more than *one* chicken wearing a chef's hat decorated with big red hearts somewhere in this blasted mall.

Scowling furiously, he glanced at his wristwatch. Nearly time. So much for having a leisurely snack while waiting for Elizabeth. At this rate he'd be lucky to find the damned coffee bar before the wedding.

A logical voice in his head told him he should just find a directory kiosk. He seemed to recall seeing one...somewhere. But that went sorely against the grain. Of course, he could simply ask someone for directions. He shook his head at the thought. No. He'd made his brag. He'd told Elizabeth that he could find his way through this overpriced maze, and blast it, that's just what he was going to do.

He still had five full minutes. Plenty of time. He would not be beaten by a shopping mall!

"Excuse me, private," a soft voice said from behind him.

Private? He stiffened at the insult, turned around and looked down into the sharp green eyes of a woman at least seventy years old. Her silvery hair was permed and sprayed into submission, and her bright pink sweatshirt had the words Mall Walker emblazoned across the front. He assumed the term had nothing in common with another well-known phrase... *street walker*.

"Yes, ma'am?" he asked.

"Don't you look handsome?" she said softly, with a slow shake of her head. "My, I always *did* love a Marine uniform better than just about anything...."

"Thank you, ma'am," he started, already looking for a chance to get away. He had only five minutes to find that coffee shop. Harding glanced at the short woman planted firmly in front of him. What was it about a uniform that got people talking?

"You know, my dear late husband, Edgar, was a Marine."

"Yes, ma'am?" He gave a mental sigh and wondered how he would be able to escape without hurting the woman's feelings. He didn't want to be rude, but he simply didn't have the time to listen to a stream of memories from a military admirer.

"Oh my, yes. He was a private, too."

He winced inwardly at the slap at his rank. It couldn't hurt to straighten her out a little. "Actually ma'am, I'm a Sergeant Major."

"No matter." She waved one hand at him and gave him a small smile. "My Edgar was a part of D Day, you know."

"Really?" People streamed past him like a swiftly moving river rushing past a rock. A rock buried deep in the mud and moving nowhere. Fast. He resisted looking at his watch again.

"Oh, yes. Why, if it hadn't been for my Edgar, who knows what might have happened on that horrible day." She paused, and when he didn't prompt her, she added, "World War II? D Day? The Normandy Invasion? Surely they teach privates about World War II these days."

"Yes, ma'am," he said, and bit down on the inside of his cheek to keep from smiling wryly. "I believe it's been mentioned a time or two."

"Well, thank heavens. I'd hate to think Edgar's sacrifice was in vain, you know."

Sacrifice? Immediately contrite that he hadn't given her his complete attention, he told himself that the widow of a fellow Marine deserved better. Quietly Harding said, "I'm sorry ma'am. He died at Normandy, then?"

She jerked her head back and stared at him, horrified. "I should say not! Why he's at the Golf Pro shop this very minute."

Now he really *was* lost. "But you said 'his sacrifice'?"

She frowned at him. "My Edgar was deathly ill at the time...his sinuses have always been a source of travail for the dear man...yet he put his own misery aside in order to drive the men to the harbor where they boarded the ships to mount the invasion. If not for my Edgar—" she shook her head slowly "—why, everything might have turned out differently."

Oh, for— Giving her a polite nod, he sent his best to Edgar and made his escape as quickly as possible. Pick a direction. Any direction. Some pathfinder, he told himself. Yet in his own defense, he had to admit that the people now rushing through familiar territory would be completely lost in a jungle. He, on the other hand, would shine in such a situation.

He glanced at his watch and grumbled in irritation. Eleven thirty-five. Shifting his gaze to sweep across the crowded mall, he was almost ready to cry defeat and look for a directory when he had a better idea.

Casually he strolled toward a group of four teenage girls and stopped just a foot or two short of them. Then he wondered aloud, "Now where was that coffee bar?"

One of the girls giggled and elbowed her friend who was staring at Harding in wide-eyed appreciation. "Are you looking for Lola's Latte?" the giggler asked.

Lola? Latte? "Would that be the coffee bar on the second level?" he asked, just to make sure.

"That's the one," another girl piped up.

"Then, yes," Harding told them. "I am looking for Lola's." He swallowed what was left of his pride and asked, "Do you know where it is?"

"Sure," the giggler spoke up again, pushed past her friends and sidled up close to Harding.

She couldn't have been more than seventeen, so he took a hasty step back. Quite a day. First Grandma, then a kid.

"Go right along here," the girl said, "turn right at the Pokey Puppy, go past the Discovery store and Lola's is right next to Potato Pete's."

Potato, Pokey, Discovery, he had to get out of this place. "Thanks, ladies," he said, and started moving, ignoring the giggler's heavy sigh as he brushed past her. He was already late, but if he hurried, maybe he'd get lucky. Maybe Elizabeth had gotten held up at the dress shop. Maybe he would still beat her to their appointment.

Then again, maybe not.

He slowed down purposely when he saw her sitting at a small round table outside Lola's, leisurely sipping from an oversize yellow coffee cup. Bad enough that he was late. No sense in looking like he was running.

In the instant before she saw him, Harding took a long minute to appreciate the picture she made.

No one should be able to look as good in jeans as she did in black silk. But somehow, Elizabeth managed it. Those worn, faded Levi's of hers hugged her long, slender legs like the hands of a familiar lover. Her tight blue T-shirt clung to her full breasts, defining a figure made to drive a man crazy. She shook her soft brown hair back from her face, and her gold hoop earrings glinted in the sunshine spilling in from the overhead skylight.

Harding gritted his teeth. He'd already had one

long, sleepless night, thanks to memories of her and the kisses they'd shared on a moonlit beach. Studying her in such close detail wasn't helping any.

She spotted him and raised a hand to wave at him. He swallowed the groan rising in his chest as his gaze locked on the smooth expanse of lightly tanned skin exposed between the hem of her shirt and the waistband of her jeans.

He walked to the coffee bar as quickly as he could, ignoring the ache in his groin caused by just the sight of her. He had the distinct feeling that as long as he was around Elizabeth Stone, he wouldn't be walking in comfort.

A smile curved one corner of her mouth as he dropped into the chair opposite her. Glancing first at her watch, she looked at him through amused brown eyes. "Eleven forty-five, Sergeant Major."

"I know." He shifted in the chair, set the Macy's bag on the table and tried to ignore the tantalizing temptation of her luscious mouth.

She grinned, and something inside him tightened.

"Lost?" she asked.

"No," he corrected. "Just...delayed."

"Uh-huh," Elizabeth nodded, set her cup down and signaled for the waiter. Looking back at Harding, she asked, "Would you like a cup of coffee? A compass? Or perhaps just a knife and a piece of string?"

The glimmer of amusement in her eyes couldn't be ignored. Neither could the knot of need centering low in his belly. Humiliating as it was to admit, he wanted her more than anything. Even her laughter at his ineptness wasn't enough to quash the desire building within him.

Determined to ignore the direction his thoughts were taking, he forced a smile and admitted, "Coffee would be great. And if you're going to leave me alone in this place again...a compass wouldn't be out of line."

Elizabeth looked surprised, then a short chuckle rippled past her throat and settled over him. Reaching across the table, she lightly laid her hand atop his.

"Congratulations, Harding. You're the first man I've ever known to admit to being lost."

He looked down at their joined hands. Jagged streaks of heat stabbed at him. Lifting his gaze, he met hers and saw the same staggering sense of awareness reflected in her eyes.

Immediately she pulled her hand back and buried it in her lap.

A waiter silently came up to the table.

And the moment was lost.

But Harding had a feeling that during the next week with Elizabeth, there would be plenty of such moments.

Five

That was a mistake.

Under cover of the tabletop, Elizabeth rubbed the fingers of her right hand together. It did no good, though. Her flesh still tingled as if she'd received a small electrical shock.

She should have known better than to touch him. Hadn't the memory of his kisses kept her up half the night? Yes, but by the time dawn had streaked across the sky, she had managed to convince herself that she had imagined her strange, overpowering reaction to Harding Casey. So much for that theory.

"Elizabeth?" he asked. "Are you all right?"

No. Definitely not. "Sure," she said, forcing a lightness she didn't feel into her tone. "I'm fine."

"Then, you don't want another cup of coffee?" he

asked, nodding his head toward the impatient-looking waiter standing alongside their table.

Lord. Apparently a simple touch of Harding's hand could send her into a zombielike state where she didn't even hear conversations going on around her. How long had the two of them been waiting for her attention?

"Actually," she said, pushing her nearly empty cup to one side. "I'd love another, thanks."

Harding nodded at the young man, who shook his head in exasperation before picking up her cup and moving off.

"So where were you?" he asked when they were alone again.

"What do you mean?" Dumb. She knew exactly what he meant.

He smiled knowingly. "Your body was here, but your mind was someplace else entirely. Thinking up new recipes?"

"All right. I mean, yes." It was better than anything she could come up with at the moment.

He nodded slowly. "I guess your ideas must come to you all the time."

"Oh, yes," she answered honestly. "My imagination is always active." Way *too* active at times, but she didn't need to tell him that.

"Mike tells me that you're making the wedding cake."

With the conversation moving to safe ground, Elizabeth smiled and breathed a sigh of relief. "I couldn't let my own sister get married with just any old cake, could I?"

"No, I suppose not." He folded his large, callused hands together on the bright yellow tabletop. "Still, it's a lot of work, isn't it?"

Elizabeth, despite her best intentions, was staring at those hands of his, imagining what it would be like to feel them moving over her flesh. Stroking. Caressing. Exploring.

"Elizabeth?"

"Hmm?" She snapped out of her dangerous daydream and caught his wary stare.

"Are you *sure* everything's all right?"

"I'm fine, Sergeant Major," she said firmly, determined to get past this ridiculous fascination she had for him. "As to the cake—" she sincerely *hoped* they had still been talking about the cake when she zoned out "—it will take some time, but it will be worth it."

"I can hardly wait to taste it," he said softly.

Unwillingly her gaze shifted to his mouth. A slow chill slithered up her spine, and she shivered. Thankfully, the waiter chose just that moment to appear, drinks in hand.

Setting them down in front of her and Harding, the young man gave her another glance, then moved away quickly.

Terrific. Even strangers were noticing her odd behavior. What had happened to all of the strong words she'd thrown at him the night before? Wasn't she the one who had said that she could outlast any Marine? Wasn't she the one who had said that spending a week with him wouldn't bother her in the slightest?

Well, it had only been two days, and not only was she bothered, she was *hot* and bothered.

"So," Harding asked, picking up the fire-engine red cup, "what am I having?"

"I beg your pardon?"

"I told him to bring me one of whatever you were drinking. It seemed easier than trying to decipher that menu."

She smiled. True, there were far too many different types of drinks listed on the chalkboard over the counter. Being a creature of habit, Elizabeth always ordered the tried and true. "It's café mocha."

He raised his cup to his lips, sniffed, smiled and tasted. "It's good."

"Darn right," she said, taking a sip herself. "It's chocolate. Hard not to be good."

"Mike told me you were a fanatic about chocolate."

"*Fanatic* is a hard word."

"But appropriate?"

She smiled. "Definitely."

"And is the wedding cake chocolate?"

"On the inside, you bet. The outside will be traditional white…with a few surprising elements."

"A lot like the chef, then. Traditional, but with surprises."

"What do you mean?"

He reached across the table and captured one of her hands. Instantly a jolt of electricity skittered up the length of her arm. Judging by the flash of awareness in his eyes, Harding had felt it, too.

"That's what I'm talking about," he said softly.

"Every time I touch you, I feel it. Something out of the ordinary. Something surprising. Startling."

She pulled her hand free, not because she wanted to, but because it was the only prudent move. "I thought we decided last night, that this...*thing* between us wasn't going to go anywhere."

"I know what we said." He spoke softly, keeping his already-deep voice pitched to a level that made her think of moonlight. Firelight. Naked passion. "But this is damned hard to ignore."

"We have to try." She held her coffee cup in both hands and took a long sip before continuing. "Look, Harding," she said, "we're not kids. We don't have to give in to what is basically just a hormonal urge." Just the thought of surrender, though, brought another chill to her spine.

"Is that all it is?" he whispered.

"It's all it can be." She pulled a deep breath into her lungs and prayed that her voice would be steady when she spoke again. "Neither one of us is interested in a relationship. You're a career Marine—and though there's nothing *wrong* with that—"

"Gee, thanks."

"I grew up in the military. I've had enough."

"I didn't ask you to marry me."

She blushed. Dammit, she could feel heat and color race up her neck and blossom in her cheeks. Served her right. He *hadn't* suggested any long-term relationship. All he had talked about was their obvious attraction for each other. Hardly a declaration of undying love, for goodness' sake.

What was wrong with her, anyway? She hadn't felt

so clumsy and nervous around a man since she was seventeen. And this was no time to lose her sense of balance.

"You're right." Elizabeth forced a choked laugh past the knot in her throat. "You didn't. And if you had, I would have said no."

Something flickered in his eyes, but was gone before she could identify it. He nodded slowly, his mouth grim. "So, what's the problem with talking about whatever this is that's going on between us?"

"It's pointless, Harding," she said. "And dangerous."

"How do you figure?" His index finger curled through the handle of the coffee cup. He lifted it, took a drink and waited for her answer.

"Neither one of us wants this relationship to last beyond Mike and Terry's wedding, right?"

"Yeah, but—" he shrugged again and set the cup down "—we'll probably be seeing each other off and on for years as we visit them."

Years. Years of torture. Years of watching him. Wanting him. Swell.

"All the more reason to stop this before it starts," she told him briskly. "If we were to give in to this…*thing*, imagine how awkward the situation would be every time we met."

One corner of his mouth turned up in a half smile. Damn. Why did he have to be so good-looking? Why couldn't Mike's best friend have been a one-eyed troll with a bad leg?

"You don't think this is awkward already?"

"Difficult, not awkward. Awkward is making polite conversation with someone you've seen naked."

Now she couldn't mistake the emotion flaring up in his eyes. Desire. Instantaneous, combustible desire. She recognized it immediately, because she was feeling the same thing. Just the thought of Harding Casey, naked, invading her body with his own, was enough to start small tingles of expectation thrumming in her center. She shifted uncomfortably in the seat.

A long, tension-filled minute passed before Harding tore his gaze from hers. "You're right," he said.

"I am?" She cleared her throat. "About what in particular?"

"About this. Talking about it. Thinking about it. It's pointless. Not to mention frustrating as hell." He stood up abruptly. Checking the total on their check, he pulled a bill from his pants pocket, tossed it onto the table and said, "We'd better get going, Elizabeth." Picking up their packages, he held his free hand out to her, to help her up.

She stared at it for a long moment, then lifted her gaze to his. If she put her hand in his, the flames would ignite, and they would be right back where they started.

"Oh," he said, finally understanding her hesitation. "Yeah. Okay." His hand fell to his side, and he stepped back, giving her plenty of room to walk past him into the milling crowds.

Safety in numbers, Elizabeth told herself. As long as they surrounded themselves with people, neither of them would be tempted to give in to what they both really wanted.

A long, hot, incredibly satisfying night of love-making.

Mentally grasping for a change in subject, she blurted, "What else has Mike told you about me?"

Anaheim Stadium was crowded. Too early in the season for the Angels' die-hard fans to be disgusted at yet another lost chance at the Pennant, the stands were filled with people telling each other that this year would be *the* year.

Harding looked to his right briefly. Mike and Terry were so wrapped up in each other, they probably hadn't noticed that the game was half-over. Shifting his gaze, he looked at the woman sitting on his left. Three days. He'd only known her for three days...and yet, it felt like forever. He hardly remembered a time when he hadn't had the image of her soft brown eyes in his mind. Her scent haunted him and every moment spent with her was a strange combination of pleasure and torture.

No woman had ever affected him like this.

Elizabeth made a notation on the score book page of the program laying across her lap, then shouted at the home plate umpire.

"If you can't see any better than that, I'll give you a ride home. You shouldn't be driving!"

Harding suppressed a chuckle and only half heard the man sitting behind them mutter, "You tell 'im, lady!"

Who would have guessed that Elizabeth Stone, the Princess of Party Cooking, was such a rabid baseball fan? Sure, Mike had told him that she enjoyed the game…but she actually kept score. Not just listing home runs, but pitcher substitutions, pinch runners…everything.

He smiled to himself as she reached up to push her hair behind her ears. Her gold hoop earrings winked in the glare of the overhead stadium lights. Harding curled his fingers into his palms to keep himself from touching her. All day, every day, he had been quelling that impulse. And it wasn't getting any easier.

His body tightened. He clenched his jaw at the discomfort. A discomfort he was becoming all too accustomed to.

He stood up abruptly, and Elizabeth looked at him.

"I'm going for something to eat," he said, more gruffly than he had intended. "You want anything?"

She glanced at Mike and Terry. Her sister was leaning in to accept her fiancé's kiss. Muttering under her breath, Elizabeth stood, laid her program on her seat and said, "I'll come with you."

So much for getting a little distance, he told himself. Glancing over his shoulder, he asked, "Mike. You two want anything?"

Mike didn't even look up. He just shook his head and kissed Terry again. Grumbling softly, Harding stepped out onto the stepped aisle and followed Elizabeth to the upper level. He tried to keep his gaze from locking onto the seductive sway of her bottom in those worn jeans. But he failed.

The line at the snack bar was ten people deep. They joined the crowd silently, Harding standing directly in back of her. An inch or so of space separated them, and still he could feel the heat emanating from her and taunting him with her nearness.

Where had all of his resistance gone? What had happened to the man who had insisted that he could spend a week in this woman's company without giving in to desire? Humph. The answer was easy. Three days into the week, that fool of a man was discovering that he was feeling something *more* than desire. Something that wouldn't be ignored and apparently had no intention of going away.

"Enjoying the game?" she asked over the noisy hum of the crowd.

"Not as much as you are," he said. Conversation was good. Maybe talking would help keep his mind too occupied for dangerous daydreams.

She glanced at him over her shoulder and smiled. "Baseball was the one thing my father and I shared. We never stayed in one place long enough to call any team 'ours,' so we always cheered for the Yankees. Since I moved to California, I've finally got a home team to root for. The Angels beak my heart annually, but I won't give up on them."

"Never surrender?"

"Exactly."

The crowd moved as one, inching closer to the snack counter. Mingled scents of popcorn, roasting hot dogs and beer floated in the air.

Someone jostled Elizabeth, pushing her backward, into Harding. Her bottom brushed against his already aching groin, and he sucked in a gulp of air in response. He grabbed her upper arms and held her still. If she moved again, he was a dead man.

"Harding," she muttered, pressing herself closer against him. "This isn't working."

"Tell me about it." His teeth ground together when she leaned into him.

"I'll never last out the week."

He dipped his head to whisper in her ear. "Me, either."

She shivered slightly as his breath brushed across her skin. He dropped one hand to her waist. Sliding his arm around her front, he held her tightly to him.

Elizabeth let her head fall back onto his chest. Her eyes closed as she concentrated on the feel of his hard readiness pressed against her bottom. She shifted her hips slightly and felt his quick intake of breath.

"How hungry are you?" he whispered, once more tickling her flesh with his breath.

She licked suddenly dry lips. It didn't matter that they were standing in the middle of a rowdy crowd. If anything, that fact only made their private dance more exciting. Dangerous.

During the last few moments, she had forgotten all about the baseball game, the snack bar, even her sister and Mike, still sitting in the stands. For now, all she knew or cared about was the man holding her. The man whose touch electrified her. The man she wanted more than she wanted her next breath.

It was pointless to deny this attraction. This desire. Even now the flames of passion were licking at her center, stirring her senses into a whirlwind of need that threatened to choke off her air.

"I'm not hungry, Harding," she answered softly. "Not for a hot dog, anyway."

"Then let's get out of here," he muttered thickly. Keeping one arm around her waist, he guided her through the crowd until they were clear. He kept walking until they were half-hidden behind a concrete pillar.

Every breath strained her lungs to the bursting point. Elizabeth looked up into his eyes, then lifted one hand to cup his cheek. "This is crazy, Harding. We've only known each other three days."

He turned his face into her hand, kissing the palm. Lifting one hand, he captured hers and squeezed it before saying, "We *met* three days ago. But we've heard about each other for a year now."

"Still..." She shook her head, some rational corner of her mind trying to deny what was happening.

"I know your favorite color is blue," he whispered. "You hate cats, love dogs and always wanted three children—two boys and a girl."

She swallowed heavily before speaking. "I know you have no family beyond the Corps. You kill plants by overwatering them, and you like your coffee black with two sugars."

He gave her a slow, lopsided smile. "We're not strangers, Elizabeth. From the moment we met, I knew this was where we were headed."

Her heartbeat skittered, then accelerated, slamming against her rib cage. Every inch of her body felt as though it was on fire. She ran the pad of her thumb across his lips, and when his tongue darted out to taste her flesh, she gasped, feeling the intimate caress down to the soles of her feet.

"I knew it, too, Harding," she managed to say. "And I don't want to fight it anymore."

He groaned slightly and moved in even closer to her, until they were both hidden in the shadows. "Fighting's not what I have in mind," he whispered. Then he dipped his head and claimed her mouth for the kiss they'd both been waiting for.

She sagged against him, offering herself up to the flames of desire raging through her. His tongue parted her lips and swept inside her mouth, stealing what was left of her breath and charging her with a hum of energy that lit up her insides like a fireworks display.

Time stopped. His fingers speared through her hair at the sides of her head and held her still for his gentle assault on her senses. Every stroke of his tongue brought new sensations, sharper pangs of need. She met him, touch for touch, caress for caress, their tongues twining together in an ancient dance of desire.

A distant roar of applause and cheers from the stadium crowd finally broke them apart, reminding them both where they were. Harding took a half step backward, clearly reluctant to leave her.

"I'll go back to our seats," he said softly. "Tell Mike and Terry that you're not feeling well. I'm going to take you home."

She nodded, her throat too full to speak, her emotions too near the surface. She could still taste him. Running her tongue lightly over her lips, Elizabeth shivered as his gaze followed the sultry motion. There was no way she would be able to simply sit and watch a baseball game. Not now. Not when her body was alive with expectation.

"Wait here," he told her. "I'll be back in a minute."

He turned, took a step, then stopped. Looking back at her, Harding stared directly into her eyes for a long, slow minute. Finally he asked, "Are you sure this is what you want, Elizabeth?"

There it was. Her chance to call a halt to this insanity that had overtaken them. With the word *No* she knew Harding would escort her back to her seat, and they could go on as they had been…each pretending that this magic between them didn't exist. Each trying to forget what had happened in the past few stolen moments.

"Hurry back, Harding," she whispered brokenly, making the only decision she could.

Six

The twenty-five-minute drive from the stadium to her condo had never seemed so long before. Freeway miles flew past, but once on the side streets, they were caught by every red light.

Elizabeth shifted in the Mustang's bucket seat and shot a glance at the man beside her. Immediately, her stomach began to pitch and turn. She wasn't regretting her decision—but the strained silence arching between them made the whole situation a bit…strange. She'd never known such passionate urgings before she'd met Harding Casey. But then, she'd never known a man like him before, either.

Spirals of need curled within her, prompting another uncomfortable shift in her seat. Her favorite jeans felt too tight. Too constraining. The seat belt slashing across her front pressed against her breasts, increasing the ache already planted by want. She bit her lip and groaned her frustration when yet another red light stopped them only a few blocks from her condo.

"Think somebody's trying to tell us something?" Harding asked tightly.

She looked at him sharply. Was *he* regretting their hasty decision to leave the ballpark for her house?

"Changing your mind, Harding?" Somehow, she squeezed those words past the knot in her throat, then held her breath as she waited for his answer.

He turned his head to look at her, and she knew immediately that nothing had changed. Even in the darkness his eyes seemed to burn with the same fires streaking through her. His right hand dropped from the steering wheel. He reached across the automatic gearshift, laying his palm on her left leg. Slowly, firmly, he stroked her thigh. She felt the heat of his touch slip through the worn denim fabric and sink down into her bones. She held her breath as his hand moved to her inner thigh.

"What do you think, Elizabeth?" he asked quietly, shifting his hand until his fingers cupped her aching center.

Breath rushed from her lungs. She stared into his eyes and saw her own need and hunger reflected back at her. His fingers smoothed up and down over the denim stretched across the joining of her thighs. His gaze held hers, refusing to let her look away. The lake blue of his eyes darkened with every ragged breath she drew, and when she parted her legs farther, she watched his features tighten.

The driver behind them honked his horn, demanding they notice that the light had turned green. Elizabeth squelched a groan threatening to erupt from her chest. She didn't want him to stop touching her. She suddenly couldn't bear the thought of not having his hands on her.

Harding scowled into his rearview mirror and stepped on the gas. He guided the responsive car with one hand on the wheel. Though he kept his eyes on the road, his right hand continued to torture Elizabeth. As if responding to a need as deep as her own, he didn't break the contact between them.

She let her head loll against the seat back, and she closed her eyes to the streetlights whizzing past. In the enclosed shelter of his car, it was as though the entire world had disappeared, leaving only the two of them.

As the Mustang slowed down again, she thought she heard him mutter a curse, but she wasn't sure. She wasn't sure of anything beyond the incredible sensation of his fingers moving on her body.

The Mustang's engine hummed as they waited out another red light. Elizabeth turned her head and opened her eyes to look at him. Their gazes locked and held as she felt his nimble fingers undoing the button fly of her jeans.

"Harding," she whispered, suddenly all too aware of the cars behind and alongside them. True, it was dark, but what if someone saw them anyway? "You can't—"

"I already have," he countered, and slid his fingertips down over her abdomen and beneath the band of her panties.

"Oh, my," she gasped and lifted her hips, unconsciously helping him toward his goal.

"Oh, Elizabeth," he said softly. His fingertips slowly caressed her damp heat—without the barrier of her jeans.

Embarrassed, excited and tortured almost to the breaking point, she looked away from him, directing a blank stare toward the traffic streaming across the intersection in front of them. Dangerous, her mind screamed. Scandalous.

She was allowing a man to make love to her while they sat at a red light on Beach Boulevard. What was worse, she had no intention of stopping him.

What was happening to her? Where was the safe, sane woman she had always been? She grabbed the armrest, curling her fingers into the padded black vinyl. The stream of traffic in front of her blurred. Half closing her eyes, she bit down hard on her bottom lip to keep from crying out at his tender, intimate touch.

"Not much farther," he said as the light turned green and they were able to go again.

She nodded, swallowed, then heard herself say, "Hurry, Harding. Hurry."

His fingertips found her most sensitive spot. Unable to help herself, she moaned softly and spread her legs wider in response. She lifted her hips off the seat slightly, instinctively trying to draw him in farther. But the strong denim fabric would only give so far.

Frustration and expectation warred within her. She glanced at him again and noted the taut lines of strain etched into his face. Shifting for a quick look at her surroundings, Elizabeth saw that they were only a block or two from her house now.

So close.

And still so far.

She leaned toward him as far as her seat belt would allow. Harding shot her a look from the corner of his eye as she came nearer.

"Elizabeth?"

The deep rumble of his voice filled the car, but she didn't answer him. Instead, she laid one hand on his powerfully muscled thigh and felt it tighten reflexively. His fingers clenched around the steering wheel. Running her palm lightly up and down the inside of his thigh, she tried to share the incredible sensations he was showering on her. Her fingers brushed across his groin as he made the left turn into her condominium complex.

He muttered something unintelligible as he reluctantly pulled his hand free of her jeans and maneuvered the car into a parking slot in front of her condo. Yanking on the emergency brake, he turned off the engine, snatched the keys out of the ignition, then got out of the car. She fumbled with the buttons on her jeans and still had her own door open before he arrived.

Reaching into the car, he helped her out, kept a tight hold on her hand and marched up the flower-lined walkway to her front door, Elizabeth stepping quickly to keep up with him.

She tried to get the key into the dead-bolt lock three times before Harding took it from her, slid it home and turned it, opening the door in a rush. They stepped inside, he slammed the door, set the lock again and grabbed for her.

Elizabeth clutched at his shoulders in the dimly lit foyer. His hands were everywhere. Touching, caressing. He lifted the hem of her shirt and dragged it up and over her head. She shook her hair back from her face and reached for the buttons on his uniform.

"This is crazy," she whispered as the last button was freed.

"Completely nuts," he agreed, shrugging out of his shirt, then pulling his white undershirt off as well.

"We're not thinking," she muttered, and gasped as his knuckles brushed her skin. He undid the front clasp of her bra, then pushed it off her shoulders so he could admire her breasts unhampered. "We should be thinking."

"Probably," he said, lifting one of her breasts and rubbing his thumb across the distended nipple.

"Ohh...." She moaned helplessly, took his free hand and placed it on her other breast. Shudders wracked her body as ribbons of pleasure swirled through her. "What if we regret this tomorrow, Harding?"

He bent his head, drew one nipple into his mouth and slowly, lovingly, circled it with his tongue. After too brief a time, he straightened again. "It'd still be worth it," he whispered.

Lifting her hands to his broad, naked chest, her fingers entwined themselves in the dark hair sprinkled across his flesh. His shining, silver dog tags tinkled musically as she stroked his skin. Her thumbs dusted over his flat nipples, and he groaned, grabbing her to him tightly.

Sliding his fingers into her hair, he tipped her head back and held her for his kiss. His mouth came down on hers like a dying man who'd been offered a last drink of water. His tongue plundered her mouth, taking all she had to offer and silently demanding more.

Everything in her was on fire. She felt the rush of passion building into an inferno and gave herself over to the flames. Clutching at him, she dug her fingernails into his shoulders and hung on as if he was the only steady point in her universe. Whatever it was that lay between them, it was more powerful than anything she had ever known. Though her mind still worried about what she was doing, her body knew it was right.

She twisted slightly in his arms, rubbing her breasts against his chest, loving the feel of her own soft flesh brushing over his hard muscles. She luxuriated in the feel of his strong arms wrapped around her bare back. Then one of his hands dropped to her behind, pulling her tightly to his hard readiness, and she groaned again, louder this time.

She needed him now.

She had to feel him entering her body, becoming one with her.

"Harding," she gasped as she broke their kiss.

"Now," he muttered, and buried his face in the curve of her neck and shoulder.

"Yes," she whispered. "Upstairs. First door."

He lifted her easily, and she didn't even have time to enjoy the sensation of being carried before he set her on her feet beside the queen-size bed. He took a step back and tore at his belt buckle.

Frantic now, Elizabeth unbuttoned her jeans and pushed them and her panties down her legs, only to be stopped by her running shoes. Hurriedly she toed her shoes off, then kicked off her pants. She turned to face him and stared silently. He was more amazing than she had expected. Tall and muscular, his body was a testament to the rigorous training of the Marine Corps.

Her gaze dropped to his groin, and she felt a momentary pang of worry when she realized how large and ready he was.

But then he came to her, sweeping her into the circle of his arms and laying her down onto the mattress. And at once, the inferno between them leaped into life again. She parted her legs as he moved over her and positioned himself between her thighs. She felt the featherlight touch of his hands smoothing up and down the insides of her legs. The tips of his fingers explored her most tender flesh, dipping in and out of the moist heat of her body until Elizabeth was ready to shatter into a million tiny pieces.

"Harding," she gasped, looking up into his darkened blue eyes. "Harding, I need..."

"Just what I need, Elizabeth," he finished for her, and came up on his knees. Slipping his hands beneath her, he lifted her hips slightly and drove himself home.

She arched into him, her head digging into the mattress, her arms up, blindly reaching for him. He shifted, moving his hands to the mattress on either side of her head. Bracing himself, he leaned over her, stared down into her wide eyes and moved within her.

Over and over, he retreated and advanced, hurtling them both ever closer to the mindless explosion of sensation awaiting them. She felt it building, humming along her nerve endings, toying with her. Teasing her with its nearness. Her fingers clenched tightly behind his neck, she rocked her hips in time with his, their dance racing to its conclusion.

When the first tremor shook her, she held him tighter, closer. Taking a deep breath, she threw herself over the edge of caution and into the whirlpool of release. Each rippling explosion of satisfaction rocked her harder than the one before. She cried out as her pleasure crested, and held him tighter still when he stiffened, moaned her name and emptied himself inside her.

Harding had never known anything like it. His groin ached with satisfaction, and already, a new, stronger need was rising up within him. The blood rushed through his veins and his own heartbeat thundered in his ears.

She moved beneath him, and he immediately levered himself up onto his elbows.

"Don't," she said quickly.

"Don't what?"

"Don't pull away yet."

His body hardened and thickened inside her. Her damp, tight warmth surrounded him, and he felt as though he would never leave the sanctuary he had found. Instinctively he rocked his hips against her, showing her without words that he had no intention of pulling away from her.

Her hands slid up and down his back, and everywhere she touched came alive. Her palms dusted his flesh and he groaned quietly. "I want you again," he whispered, and bent to take one of her nipples into his mouth.

She arched against him, and he grazed the distended bud with the edges of his teeth. His tongue worked her nipple, circling, flicking at the tender flesh with short strokes.

"This can't be happening again," she said on a half sigh. "So soon..."

"Again," he whispered as he lifted his head and looked down into her eyes. "And again and again. I can't get enough of you, Elizabeth. The taste of you, the feel of you." He pushed his body deeper inside her, enjoying the sparkle of pleasure he saw flickering in her eyes. She wanted him as badly as he did her. That knowledge fed the flames of his own passion.

Harding wrapped his arms around her, and when he eased himself up onto his haunches, he kept her with him, his body buried within her. She straddled him, her legs on either side of his thighs. Wiggling her hips slightly, she took him even deeper inside as his hands dropped to her hips.

Her head fell back, and Harding looked his fill of her. In the moonlight streaming through the second-story window, her brown hair glimmered and shone. Curls fell in a tangled mass around her head, and her gold hoops swung in abandon, making her look like some ancient, pagan goddess—naked but for the gold at her ears.

His hands encompassed her narrow waist briefly before he allowed one of his hands to slide down her abdomen to the nest of pale brown curls at the juncture of her thighs. She tensed, waiting. He smiled to himself and stroked her most sensitive spot.

She straightened up on his lap, shifting her hips from side to side, cradling his body with hers. Her hands at his shoulders, she bent to claim his mouth, and this time he let her be the aggressor. She branded him with strokes of her tongue, stealing his breath and giving him hers.

Unable to wait another moment, Harding placed both hands on her hips. Then, guiding her, he helped her move on him. Each time she took him inside her, he felt his world shift. When completion roared toward them, he clamped his mouth to hers, devouring her sighs and muffling his own shout of satisfaction.

She didn't remember moving, but when she opened her eyes again, she was lying on fresh, cool sheets, the quilt pulled neatly over her.

And Harding.

She glanced down at her waist and laid one hand on the arm he had wrapped around her. Her body still humming with the lingering effects of their lovemaking, she was embarrassed to admit—even to herself— that she wanted more. Needed more.

"Awake?" he asked quietly.

"Uh-huh," she said on a sigh. "What time is it?"

"Around midnight."

Nodding, she turned in his arms until she could see him.

Bracing himself on one elbow, Harding looked down at her steadily. Somberly.

A warning sounded somewhere deep inside her. Whatever afterglow she was experiencing, Harding apparently wasn't.

"What is it?" she managed to ask.

He frowned slightly, released her long enough to rub one hand across his face, then said, "We have to talk."

Something cold slithered along her spine. She pulled the sheet up higher over her breasts, scooted a couple of inches away from him. "If you're thinking about apologizing to me, don't."

"Elizabeth…"

"I mean it, Harding." Strange how quickly a glow could disappear. Stranger still how much colder she felt now that it was gone. "We're both grown-ups. We knew what we were doing."

"Not entirely."

She pulled a bit farther away from him, pushed her hair out of her eyes and asked, "What's that supposed to mean?"

"We didn't take any precautions," he said flatly.

"Precau—" Good heavens. Her stomach dropped, and she thought she even felt her heartbeat skitter a bit as the implications of what he was saying sunk in.

Sitting up, she crossed her legs Indian style and clutched the quilt to her like a frightened virgin. Despite the situation, she almost laughed. A bit late for trying to protect her virtue.

"I don't see a damn thing funny in this," he pointed out.

"Not funny," she corrected. "Ridiculous. Embarrassing."

"Embarrassing?"

"Of course. These days, any teenager knows better than to do what we just did!"

He pushed himself off the mattress and began to pace. "I don't suppose you take the Pill?" he asked on one of his trips around the room.

"No," she said, shaking her head. "There didn't seem to be any point." Flopping back against the headboard, she frowned and admitted wryly, "I don't exactly have what you would call a busy love life."

He stopped dead and looked at her, one eyebrow lifted into a high arch.

"Sure, tonight," she shot at him. "But before you there was only—" She broke off and stared at him.

"What?"

"Is that what your concern is for? Trying to find out if I've got anything *contagious?"*

"Dammit, Elizabeth."

"Rest easy, Harding." She clumsily got out of bed, still dragging that quilt with her. Wrapping it around her, she tossed the tail end of the blanket over one shoulder, lifted her chin and said, "I'm completely safe. I've only been with one other man and—"

"One?"

A flush of heat stormed up her neck and stained her cheeks. "Apparently I've given you the wrong impression, here. Believe me, the way I acted with you tonight is not my normal behavior. I don't ordinarily hop into the sack with someone I've known for three days."

"That's not what I meant—"

"I can understand why you might not want to believe me, what with the evidence all to the contrary..."

"Elizabeth," he said, and took a step toward her.

She jumped backward. As insulting as his comment had been, she didn't trust herself if he was to touch her. Damn his eyes, anyway, she would probably melt into him and find herself flat on her back again.

He took a deep breath before speaking in a slow, too calm voice, "I didn't mean that. I was only surprised that a woman like you—"

"Fast and loose?"

"Dammit, stop putting words in my mouth!"

Her bottom lip trembled, and she bit down on it, hard. She wasn't going to cry, blast it. Not now. Not in front of him.

Harding saw the sheen of unshed tears swimming in her eyes and cringed inwardly. Damn, he'd made a mess of this. When he'd awakened with her in his arms, he had experienced an inner peace that he had never known before. Staring down at her features while she slept, his mind had taken an incredibly wild turn.

His imagination had leaped from this one night of passion to a lifetime of promises and children. Just the thought of it had terrified him—and yet, somehow intrigued him almost as much. *That* was the moment he had realized that he'd been a careless idiot.

Children? A baby?

Hell, how could he *not* have used a damn condom? Fine, he had the excuse of being somewhat out of practice. He'd been living a practically celibate life since his divorce. One-night stands didn't interest him—and anything more might have led to a relationship. Definitely something he didn't want.

Even the threat of which he'd managed to avoid neatly.

Until Elizabeth Stone.

Gritting his teeth, he started toward her again, determined to say his piece. She backed up, her feet tangling in the quilt she clutched to her chest as if it was Superman's cape. Her balance dissolved, and she swung one arm wide, searching for a handhold. Before she could fall, Harding caught her, dragging her up tight against him.

"Let me go."

"Not yet," he said, and lifted her chin with his thumb and forefinger until she was looking at him. Those eyes of hers mesmerized him. The deep brown color shimmered beneath a teary film. He wanted to hold her, kiss her, make love to her again until they rekindled the fire between them. Instead, though, he said, "All I meant was that I couldn't believe there were so many stupid men in the world." Not that he was complaining. He much preferred the fact that there hadn't been many men in her life.

She stopped twisting and wriggling to get free.

"A woman as beautiful and warm as you should be fighting them off with a stick."

"I have," she said pointedly.

"Until me." He smiled sadly. It wasn't an easy

thing, knowing that he had allowed his hormones to rage so out of control that he'd put her at risk.

She stiffened in his arms. "Harding, let me go."

"Not until I say what I started to say before."

"Which is *what* exactly?"

The watery film in her eyes had dissipated some, to be replaced by a flash of anger. Anger, he knew, was much easier to deal with.

"Elizabeth, I wasn't worrying about diseases." Hadn't it occurred to her yet? Apparently not. He paused, still holding her gaze with his own. "I was thinking more along the lines of a *baby*."

Her jaw dropped.

"Oh, my God," she whispered.

"Is there a chance?" he asked.

"Of course there's a *chance*," she muttered, moving away from him as his hold eased up. Sitting down on the edge of the bed, she continued to talk. "Not much of one, probably. It was only the one time."

"Two times."

She flushed again. "Two."

He hadn't known that there were still women who blushed. "I'm sorry, Elizabeth, this is all my fault."

"Stop saying you're sorry," she snapped.

"What?"

"I mean it, Harding." Glaring up at him, she went on. "Tonight happened because we *both* wanted it. You're in the clear, Sergeant Major."

The clear? Did she expect him to disappear? Leave her to pay whatever consequences might arise because of tonight? A strong surge of anger shot through him. "What the hell does that mean?"

"That means that if I hear another apology from you, I'll scream." She scooted back onto the bed, wrapped in the cocoon of her quilt. "Will you please leave, now?"

He inhaled sharply and blew the air out of his lungs in an exasperated rush. Staring at her, he saw that she had closed herself off from him as effectively as if she had slammed a door in his face. There wouldn't be any talking to her tonight. Not if he expected her to listen. *Really* listen.

Fine then. They could talk tomorrow. When she would hopefully be reasonable. Bending down, he snatched at his clothes and hurriedly pulled them on. Glancing at her, he noted that she kept her gaze averted.

In a matter of minutes he was standing beside the bed, waiting for her to acknowledge him. Finally she shot him a look from the corner of her eye.

"We'll talk about this tomorrow. I'll call you in the morning."

"I'll call you," she countered firmly, "when I'm ready to talk about it."

Harding bent down, picked her up by the shoulders and planted a hard, quick kiss on her lips. Briefly he thought he felt her kiss him back, but then her defenses went up and she turned into a block of wood. Disappointed, he dropped her back onto the bed, turned and marched to the door. There he stopped, pointed at her and ordered, "Zero nine thirty hours, Elizabeth. You pick up the damned phone."

Seven

She pulled up to the main gate at Camp Pendleton just as dawn was streaking the sky. Sparing a quick glance for the deep rose-colored clouds, she turned her complete attention on the young Marine guard standing beside her car. She must be getting old, she thought. The kid didn't look more than nineteen. She rolled down the window.

"Can I help you, ma'am?" he asked.

Boy, she hated being called ma'am. Dismissing the distraction, she got straight to the business that had brought her to the Marine base.

"I'd like to see Sergeant Major Harding Casey, please."

"Yes, ma'am," the Marine said, his gaze drifting over a paper attached to the clipboard he carried. "Is he expecting you?"

"No," she confessed. "He's not."

"Which battalion is he with, ma'am? I'll have to call the Sergeant Major before letting you in."

Battalion. Dammit. Of course they would have to know which battalion. And which regiment. Why hadn't she thought of that? She'd been raised on Marine bases. She knew firsthand the thoroughness of the gate guards.

And she didn't have the slightest idea which battalion Harding was assigned to.

Lifting one hand, she rubbed her forehead right between her eyes. Her head was pounding, and her eyes felt gritty from lack of sleep. All night, she'd lain awake, remembering everything that had passed between Harding Casey and her. Everything from the incredible passion and closeness they'd shared, to the moment when he'd destroyed the magic by apologizing and then capping that off with an order to answer her telephone.

Just who the hell did Hard Case Casey think he was, anyway? One night of lovemaking…no matter how mind-shattering…did *not* give him authority over her.

But it *might* have given her a baby.

No, no, no. Don't even think it. The chances had to be astronomically slim. Surely the odds were with her. And yet, something inside her turned over. She had always wanted a child. Three, actually. And lately she had begun to think it would never happen. What if it *had*, now? What if she was pregnant this very moment? She glanced down at her flat belly, covered by the jeans Harding had manipulated so nicely the night before, and cautiously laid her palm protectively over it.

"Ma'am?" The young Marine cleared his throat meaningfully. "His battalion and regiment?"

"I don't know," she admitted, not sure what to do now.

He must have seen the indecision in her face because he almost smiled. "If you'll pull your car off to the side there, ma'am, I'll see what I can find out."

She did as she was told, turned the engine off and waited. Watching the Marine, she saw him step into the small cubicle inside the gate and reach for a phone. Before he could use it, though, another guard appeared from behind the building. The two men spoke in tones she couldn't quite hear, until the second Marine said loudly, with a glance in her direction, "A *woman* to see Hard Case?"

She didn't know whether to be relieved or insulted. But there was definitely a part of her delighted to hear that women weren't streaming in and out of this gate visiting Harding. Elizabeth watched the second guard grab the phone, speak to someone for a moment, then hang up. He walked to her car, briefly gave her directions to Harding's quarters, then smiled and stepped back out of her way.

As she steered her Toyota along the streets of the base, an eerie feeling began to creep over her. Though her father had never been stationed at Pendleton, the base was so much like all of the others she'd lived on, she felt almost as if she were coming home.

Memories rushed into her brain, and even the air seemed almost too thick to breathe. The drive to Har-

ding's quarters became a short, personal tour of her
past. She noticed tricycles and skateboards that had
been left out on front lawns, and immediately remembered bravely pedaling her first two-wheeler down a
sidewalk while her father ran along behind, tightly
gripping the back of the bike to keep her safe.

She saw basketball hoops and chalk-marked side-
walks, which released the memory of her, Terry and
her mother playing hopscotch on hot summer after-
noons. Shadow pictures raced through her brain as
she passed a tidy church, the PX, restaurants and the
parade grounds. All of it so familiar.

Strange, but for years, whenever she thought about
her childhood, all she remembered was the pain of
always moving around—never belonging anywhere—
constant uncertainty. Now, though, other images
reared up and demanded to be noticed. The good
times. And there had been many of them. Life on a
military base wasn't always easy. But almost in com-
pensation for the trials, came the joy of feeling as
though you were part of a huge family. A family
where each member looked out for the other. A family where arguments and old injuries were put aside
in times of need.

An unexpected sheen of tears filled her eyes, and
she was nearly blinded by the past. But she blinked
them back as she pulled up in front of the senior staff
NCO billeting barracks. Determinedly, she put her
past where it belonged. She would need all of her wits
about her during this little confrontation with Harding.

Especially since she wasn't at all sure what it was she'd come to say.

As if the thought of his name had conjured him up, a door in the barracks building opened and there he was. Standing on the threshold of his quarters with a frown on his face and his silver dog tags gleaming against his tanned flesh, he had one bare shoulder propped against the doorjamb, his arms folded across his chest. He had pulled on a pair of uniform trousers, but otherwise he was naked.

Instantly memories of the night before flitted through her already-tired brain. Elizabeth's mouth went dry, and she had to force herself to move suddenly shaky legs. Once out of the car, though, she walked directly to him without stumbling once.

She stepped past him, entering the apartment. He followed her in and silently closed the door. Taking a deep breath, she turned around slowly and her gaze collided with his.

"Good morning," he said. "Zero nine thirty already?"

"No," she snapped, refusing to rise to the sarcasm. "I had to talk to you and couldn't wait for my 'assigned time.'"

He looked mildly surprised, but he nodded and started for the kitchen. "Come on. I think we're both going to need coffee." Over his shoulder, he added, "Sorry, but I'm fresh out of café mocha."

"I'll suffer," she countered and wanted to bite her tongue. If she expected to have a civilized conversation with the man, she shouldn't start by firing a warning shot.

The kitchen was small, barely big enough for two people. Faded green curtains graced the only window and on the tiny, two-seater table, was a plastic basket filled with apples and bananas.

While he started the coffee, she walked a slow circle around that table. "Look, Harding, I think there are a few things we have to get straight."

"I agree."

"Good." That was a start, wasn't it?

Finished, he turned, propped himself against the countertop and crossed his arms over his chest again. Above the gurgle and hiss of the coffeemaker, he asked, "So who goes first? You or me?"

"Me," she said quickly. "I've been thinking about this all night."

He gave her a slow nod, but his expression was unreadable.

She stopped behind one of two ladder-back wooden chairs. Curling her fingers over the top slat, she said firmly, "What you did last night was way out of line."

He smiled wryly. "I think we established *that* much before I left."

"I'm not talking about the sex," she snapped. "I'm talking about the way you apologized, took all responsibility, then walked out."

"You asked me to leave."

She waved that comment aside for the moment. "I'm a big girl, Harding. I make my own choices, and I take responsibility for those choices myself."

"Fine."

"And," she added, "nobody *orders* me to be waiting at a telephone at a certain time and place."

"All right." He half straightened and reached up to rub one hand across his hair. "We're both to blame. Happy?"

"Yes, thanks." She sat down on the chair and waited while he poured them each a cup of coffee. When he was seated in the chair opposite her, he started talking before she could say another word.

"Look, Elizabeth," he said, and she knew she wasn't going to like whatever was coming next. "I did some thinking last night, too. And whoever is to blame, what happened last night was a mistake. A big one."

Even though she'd thought the same thing herself earlier, hearing him say it out loud sent an aching emptiness ricocheting around inside her.

"And," he went on, staring into his coffee cup as if looking for the right words, "once this wedding is over, I think it's best if we don't see each other again."

"You do?"

"Yeah." Leaving his drink untouched, he jumped up from the chair, walked the short distance to the sink, then turned around to face her. In the dish drainer behind him, there were one plate, one glass, one cup and one set of silverware left overnight to dry.

Rubbing a hand across his naked chest, he added, "There's no point. Neither one of us wants a relationship, Elizabeth. If we keep seeing each other, it'll only cause a lot of pain."

Speechless, she stared at him. Well, what had she expected? Hadn't she come to the base to tell him the same thing? Wasn't this the only reasonable solution to a situation that was already getting out of hand? Why, then, did it hurt to have him say it to her?

She took hold of her coffee cup with both hands and scrambled for something to say. "I thought Marines were supposed to be able to take pain." Did her voice really sound so soft and injured? Or was it only her imagination?

Harding crossed to her and squatted alongside her chair. Looking directly into her eyes, he said, "Yeah, we can take it. We just don't like *causing* it." Trying for a smile, he added, "Except of course, to the enemy."

How strange this all was. A week ago she had never met this man. Now she was sitting in his kitchen, talking about dissolving a relationship that didn't really exist, not knowing if she was or wasn't carrying his child.

"It's better this way, Elizabeth," he said softly and reached for one of her hands. He paused for a long moment before saying, "I deploy in less than a month."

Her gaze shot to his. Deployment. More memories rose up to kick her in the stomach. Memories of her father, gone for six months at a time. Summers missed, lonely Christmases, cards and letters and posing for pictures that Mom could send to Dad, so far away. She remembered occasional phone calls and listening to the sound of his voice, so faint and distant.

Visions of her mother, trying to be both mom and dad to Terry and her. Echoes of her mother's lonely tears when she thought her daughters were asleep. So many absences. So many missed birthdays and kisses and hugs. So many missed chances.

She swallowed back the images and forced herself to ask, "Where?"

Grimly he said, "Okinawa."

The other side of the world. In less than a month he would be thousands of miles away from her. Elizabeth nodded and pulled her hand free of his, missing the electrifying warmth of his touch even as she told herself to get used to missing it.

Unable to sit still a moment longer, she stood up and walked back into the small, neat living room. For the first time she noticed the military beige walls and carpets. So familiar and yet…so different.

Her mother had always prided herself on making all of the different quarters they'd lived in home. Photos, framed postcards, hers and Terry's artwork splashed across the refrigerator, rag rugs and always, fresh flowers. Things to let people know that a family lived there. People. Not just Marines.

Small personal touches that were sadly lacking in Harding's place.

A handful of framed photographs lined the mantel over an empty fireplace, and one lone plant stood limply in the corner. Otherwise the place might have been vacant.

Noting her observation, Harding said softly, "I don't keep a lot of *things*." She turned to look at him. "And a man alone can't have pets." He half shrugged. "When I'm deployed, who would I get to take care of a dog?"

Loneliness tinged his voice, and the sharp edge of it slashed at her. She wondered if he even knew it was there. "At least you've got a plant. Mike told me you couldn't be trusted with one."

One corner of his mouth lifted slightly. "It's on loan from First Sergeant McCoy's wife. She said the apartment needed something alive in it. She'll nurse it back to health when I ship out."

Elizabeth nodded, but her thoughts were already spinning. How different their homes were. His was empty. Hers was crammed full of things. *Things.* Not people. For years, she'd been concentrating on building the secure home she'd always longed for. She had gathered up furnishings and knickknacks as if they would be enough to anchor her. But except for Terry and an occasional visit with her parents, her life was empty of people.

A chill raced along her spine, and she shivered. Was she any better than Harding? Had she really made herself a home? Or had she only stacked her possessions high enough to hide the emptiness surrounding her?

Harding watched the play of emotions darting across her features and would have given anything to know what she was thinking. Having her arrive at the base, so unexpectedly, had been like a gift. He'd lain awake all night, thinking about her, worrying about what they might be starting, knowing he should distance himself from her and wondering how in the hell he would be able to do that without dying a little every day for the rest of his life.

How had the world managed to change so completely in so little time? And how could he ever go back to living without her?

She took a breath and it caught in her throat. A tiny, choking sound issued from her, and it was like a bayonet in his back, urging him to her. He crossed the few feet of worn carpet separating them and pulled her into his arms. She buried her face in his chest, and for several long moments Harding simply stood there, holding her. He inhaled her soft, flowery scent, drawing it deep into his lungs, as if he could keep it with him always. He stroked her short, curly hair and listened until her breathing settled into a steady rhythm again.

Looking down, he let go of her only long enough to cup her face in his hands. Smoothing his thumbs across her cheekbones, he was relieved to see she hadn't been crying. But there was something in her eyes—some change that he couldn't quite identify.

"Harding," she said softly, hesitantly, "what are we going to do?"

His gaze drifted over her features slowly, like the most loving of caresses. He would remember this moment, this woman for the rest of his life. Again, the pads of his thumbs brushed over her cheeks. His fingers brushed her hair at her temples. Soft. So soft. "I don't know, Elizabeth. I don't have any answers."

"Then let's not ask each other any more questions," she said thickly. Her palms slid up his chest, her fingertips outlining his flat nipples.

He squeezed his eyes shut at the featherlight strokes of her flesh on his. His groin tightened and he ached to be with her. Inside her.

No questions? No answers? Was that enough?

"Elizabeth," he ground out, "I'm still leaving in a month. Six months I'll be away."

She reached up and laid one hand across his mouth. "We have now, Harding. For whatever reasons, we have now."

"This will only make the leaving harder," he said, feeling that he should remind her that pain was the only possible outcome of their being together.

"But it will make the now so much easier," she said, and went up on her toes to kiss him.

Even a saint couldn't have resisted her kiss—and Harding Casey was no saint. He groaned in the back of his throat, and his arms closed around her, tightening until he felt the buttons of her jeans pressing into his belly. Slipping one hand down lower, he cupped her behind and pulled her hard against him. Another groan escaped from his throat, and he lowered his mouth to take hers.

Her lips parted for him, and his tongue swept into her warmth, claiming her, branding her with each stroke. She wrapped her arms around him, running her palms up and down his back, creating a friction of heat that shot through him with the force of a sustained artillery attack.

In seconds he was more hungry for her than he had been the night before. Now he knew what awaited him in her warmth. He had experienced the wonder of her and couldn't wait to find it again. Gasping for air, he broke their kiss, tossed her up and over his shoulder and headed for the bedroom.

As he walked, Elizabeth lavished kisses over his broad back. Then, sliding her hands down beneath the waistband of his trousers, she smoothed her palms over his behind, dragging her nails across his skin until he thought he might explode from want before he was even deep within her.

In his bedroom, Harding dipped to one side, flipped her onto his mattress and quickly helped her out of her clothes. As he stepped out of his pants, he yanked open the drawer in the bedside table and fumbled in its depths for a long minute. When he finally found one of the condoms he'd had stashed there for two years, he straightened up and slammed the drawer shut again.

This time they would do things right. This time there would be no chances taken. This time, he would care for her the way she should be cared for. He glanced at her and saw her watching him. Raking his gaze over her body, he felt his own stir and ache in readiness. He tore the foil slightly before her hand on his stopped him.

"Let me," she said and took the packet from him.

His groin tightened even further at the mental image of her hands on him, but he gritted his teeth and stood very still, waiting. She opened the packet, removed the condom and slowly positioned it over the sensitive tip of him. Harding sucked in air through clenched teeth and kept his gaze locked on her and what she was doing to him. Inch by glorious inch, she slid the fragile material down his length, smoothing and caressing as she went. When she was finished, she cupped him tenderly, her fingers stroking, exploring him. Harding's blood pounded in his veins, and his heartbeat sounded like the bass drums in the Marine Corps band.

"Enough," he growled and eased her down onto the bed. Parting her thighs, he looked his fill of her. His fingertips explored her opening, gently readying her for his entry. But her body was as tensely strung as his. She was molten heat, calling to him, urging him closer. A moment later he leaned over her and drove himself home. Her tight warmth surrounded him, and when he was buried deep within her, he allowed himself a groan of satisfaction at having found the wonder again.

Then need hammered at him as desperately as her fingernails raked across his back. Her hips lifted and fell, and her breath came hot on his neck.

Taking a handful of her hair, he pulled her head back gently, and stared down into the eyes that had been haunting him since his first sight of them.

"Whatever happens, Elizabeth, we will always have this between us. This...*magic*."

He withdrew and plunged even deeper inside her. She gasped, shuddered, met his gaze and echoed, "*Magic*."

Desire and the flames of an all-consuming passion licked at them, driving them both to the conclusion that brought them each, however briefly, peace.

Eight

"We have *got* to stop meeting like this," Elizabeth said, her body still humming with the aftershocks of their lovemaking. She hadn't intended for this to happen again. All she had wanted to do was *talk* to him.

Harding rolled to one side, stifling a deep-throated groan as he moved. Grabbing a pillow, he jammed it beneath his head. Then, glancing at her, he agreed, "Too many more of these 'talks' and I'll be a dead man."

Pushing one hand through her hair, Elizabeth scooted backward until her back was propped against the headboard. She tugged one of the rumpled sheets up over her breasts and looked at the man lying beside her.

"This is nuts, Harding," she said with a quiet laugh.

"Don't I know it." Ruefully he shook his head, stood up and walked into the bathroom. A few seconds later he joined her on the bed again. Drawing her up close to his side, he kissed the top of her head. "So much for all of our fine notions about self-control."

"I don't know what it is about you, Marine," she said, and tucked her head underneath his chin. "But every time you touch me, I tend to burst into flames."

"I'm getting a little singed myself."

"What are we supposed to do about this, Harding?"

"Enjoy it while it lasts?"

She pushed back a bit and cocked her head to look at him. "Isn't that asking for trouble?"

"Not if we remember to be more careful than we were last night."

Elizabeth settled back against him and nodded slowly. Enjoy each other. Somehow it sounded so… empty. Ridiculous, she knew. After all, they were both adults.

"Regrets?" he asked quietly.

"Not really," she answered, and knew she sounded unconvincing.

"Elizabeth," he said, "just because we can't see a future together…that doesn't mean we can't have a present."

"I know that." She shook her head gently, then pushed her hair back behind her ears. "It's only that I've never—"

"Had a lover?" he finished for her.

She smiled wryly. "You make it sound so reasonable."

"Isn't it?"

"I suppose so," she said thoughtfully. "I guess I never considered myself the take-a-lover kind of woman."

"More of a white-picket-fence type of girl?"

"No." She laughed again at the notion. "I was always too concentrated on my career to think about husbands and cute little houses and station wagons."

"Ah…" He ran one hand up and down her arm in long, soothing strokes. "Well, all of your concentration worked. You *are* the Princess of Party Cooking."

She gave his hand a playful smack.

"Isn't it what you thought it would be?" he asked. "Your career, I mean?"

"Oh, I love it," she admitted softly. "There is nothing more fun than being in a well-stocked kitchen, dreaming up some new and tantalizing dessert."

"Nothing?" he asked, letting his fingertips trail along the edge of her breast.

She sucked in a breath. "Well, *almost* nothing."

"Thank you."

"You're welcome."

"So," he said, "if your career is all you wanted it to be, and you don't particularly *want* a husband, what's wrong with having a lover?"

There was a long pause while she thought that one over. Nothing wrong with it, she supposed. But, if that were true, why did she suddenly feel so… debauched? Her traditional upbringing must be rearing its ugly head, she decided. Well, if that was all it was, she would just have to get over it. As she had when she'd first decided to have a career instead of a husband. Either that or live the life of a well-fed nun.

Making up her mind, she nodded against his chest. "You're right. There's nothing wrong with having a man in my life occasionally."

His hand on her arm stilled, then continued its gentle stroking.

Of course, she would have to give up the one little corner of her dream that she hadn't allowed herself to think of for years. Children. Lovers do not necessarily make good fathers. And 1990s or not, she didn't know if she could be a good enough single parent to risk having a child alone.

Oh, she knew lots of women were doing it these days. Most of them doing it quite well, too. But the staggering responsibility of being both mother and father was one she wasn't sure she was strong enough to carry.

Immediately she remembered the night before, the first time they'd made love and the fact that there had been no protection. Was it possible that one slip had already resulted in a child? Was she, even now, pregnant with Harding's baby?

She closed her eyes, telling herself firmly not to think about that yet. It was too early to worry. Especially since she wasn't sure if she had anything to worry about. Yet.

Imagine, all of this had come about because her sister had fallen in love.

Her mind racing, Elizabeth suddenly wondered what Mike and Terry would have to say if they could see her and Harding right now. She chuckled gently at the envisioned expression on her sister's face.

"What's so funny?"

"I was just thinking about Mike and Terry and how they worked at trying to get us together for a solid year with no success."

He laughed shortly, and the sound rumbled beneath her ear. "Yeah, all I heard about was how great we would be together."

"Me, too." She tipped her head back again to look up at him. "Can you imagine the 'I told you so's' we'd have to listen to if they found out about this?"

He pushed one hand through his short hair. "Mike would never let me forget it."

"Terry, either. She lives for this sort of thing."

"So, then," he said, cupping her cheek with one big palm, "we don't tell them?"

"My lips are sealed," she said.

"Not permanently, I hope." He smiled wickedly and wiggled both of his eyebrows.

Shaking her head, she grinned at him. "It's better if they don't know, anyway. After all, they were hoping for marriage, not—"

"A red-hot, fire-breathing affair?" he finished for her.

"Exactly." She ran the flat of her hand across his chest.

He caught her hand, holding it tightly. "But just because we don't want to get married, that doesn't mean we can't enjoy what we have for as long as we have it, right?''

"Right," she said, despite the pang of regret echoing deep inside her. Less than a month, he'd said. He was leaving in less than four weeks and would be gone for six long months. And when he returned, there was no guarantee that they would reconnect. Maybe he wouldn't even want to see her. Regret slithered through her again. Already she missed him.

She could admit, if only to herself, that she was dreading his leaving. How terrible could it be for her to have these moments with him to remember when he was gone?

"What's making you frown?" he asked.

"Nothing," she lied, and forced a smile she didn't quite feel.

"You're thinking about last night, aren't you?"

"No, I wasn't."

"We have to talk about that, Elizabeth."

"Yeah, I know," she said, and thought, Not now. Not this minute.

He sighed and held her closer. "Whatever happens, we'll work it out together."

"Harding, you don't have to worry about it, all right?" she said. "Like I told you, I'm a big girl. I can take care of myself."

"I know you can," he countered, staring down into her eyes. "But if you are pregnant, there would be someone else to consider besides yourself."

"Oh, my, a baby." Mixed emotions blended together in the depths of her soul. One minute she saw herself cuddling a newborn to her breast. She blocked the next image, refusing to entertain the notion at all. Banishing both mental pictures, she shook her head firmly. "No, it won't happen."

"When will we know for sure?"

"*I'll* know in about two weeks."

"Good. I don't ship out for three weeks yet, so we'll have time to decide what to do."

"Harding," she tried to ease away from him, but he held her tighter. "I won't try to keep you out of this, and of course you'll get a chance to give me your opinion on what I should do, but the final decision will be mine."

He was quiet for several long minutes, and Elizabeth held her breath, wondering what he would have to say. She hadn't known him long, of course. But through Mike and Terry she knew what kind of man he was. She couldn't imagine him *not* having an opinion.

Finally he inhaled sharply and blew it out in a rush. "We have two weeks. Two weeks before we know if a decision will be necessary. I suggest we wait to discuss it until we know if we have something to talk about."

She sighed her relief. Now that she was here, with him, she didn't want to ruin what time she had with him by fighting over what was still a *theoretical* baby.

Slipping one of his hands beneath the sheet she'd pulled up over her breasts, he found one of her nipples and gently teased it until she was curling into him, nearly purring with pleasure.

"Elizabeth," he whispered in her ear.

"Hmm?"

"Are we going to be spending the entire day in my bed?" He dipped his head to nibble at the base of her throat.

"Have you got some official Marine business to take care of?" she asked, tilting her head back to give him easier access.

"Nope," his tongue flicked against her pulse point. "I took this whole week off as leave time. I'm officially a free man."

"Did Terry give us chores for today?" she mumbled, and bit his shoulder gently.

"Finished the last ones yesterday." He shifted, moving down the length of her body, trailing hot, damp kisses along her flesh. "All that's left is you making the cake."

"Then, Sergeant Major, I suggest we spend the day in bed, resting up for the rest of the week."

He looked up from her abdomen and gave her a quick, wicked smile. "We stay in this bed, princess, there'll be no resting."

Elizabeth shifted on the sheets, parting her legs when he moved to kneel between them. His fingers dusted along the insides of her thighs, and she felt herself jump in response. "Princess, huh?" she murmured as his hands slid beneath her bottom. "Well, Hard Case—" she broke off and looked at him quizzically. "Why do they call you Hard Case, anyway?"

"Do you really need to know that *now?*" he asked quietly, and lifted her hips high, easing her legs into place over his shoulders.

Suddenly aware of what he was about to do, Elizabeth gasped, "Harding!"

"Just lie back, princess," he said with a knowing smile.

Then his mouth covered her, and all of her thoughts dissolved into a hazy mist of delicious sensations.

At 10:00 p.m. the night before the wedding, Elizabeth sat at her kitchen table, listening to her mother and Terry as she decorated the cake.

"I just don't understand why the bachelor party *has* to be held the night before the wedding."

"Tradition," Sally Stone told her younger daughter for the third time.

Terry stuck her index finger into the small, stainless steel bowl containing lilac-tinted frosting and winced when Elizabeth smacked her hand.

"Hey, I just wanted a taste."

Elizabeth shook her head, filled the pastry bag with the lilac confection and prepared to create rosettes. "Taste it tomorrow."

"Your sister's right," Sally said.

"Naturally." Terry gave her mother a sly grin. "Lizzie was always your favorite."

Elizabeth laughed.

"Let's not start that again," their mom said and stood up. "Anyone like a cup of tea before I send Terry to bed to get some sleep?"

The woman in question frowned. "The men are out drinking beer, and I get hot tea and an early bedtime?"

"I think we can do better than that," Elizabeth told her sister. She nodded toward the slate blue side-by-side refrigerator in the corner. "There's wine in the fridge."

Terry smiled and jumped to her feet. "How about it, Mom? Feel like giving me a grand send-off?"

The older woman looked at first one daughter, then the other. Eyes twinkling, she said, "Sure. We'll have a toast. But then, the bride goes to bed. I don't want my beautiful daughter posing for her wedding pictures with bags under her eyes."

"Okay, okay," Terry agreed, and reached into the refrigerator. She grabbed a bottle of white Zinfandel, set it on the table and crossed the wide, well-appointed kitchen. "Glasses in the same place?"

"Of course." Elizabeth kept her eyes on her job. She still had two layers to pipe rosettes on, before she could add the final flourishes to what she hoped would be a masterpiece. Naturally the job would go a lot faster if she was working as she preferred to work. Alone, with Beethoven on the CD player. But with her parents spending the weekend at her condo and Terry opting to join them for one last night of family togetherness, that wasn't an option.

"Okay, Lizzie," Terry said as she filled the third glass, "take a break. That's an order."

"Hey, if you don't want a cake at the wedding," she teased, "just say so. It's all right with me."

"One minute, master chef. One minute to give your baby sister a toast."

Elizabeth sighed, set the pastry bag down onto the table and picked up her glass. Standing, she looked at the other women, each in turn. Terry looked wonderful, eager and happy. Their mother was still beautiful, even though there was more gray in her hair than blond these days. Those blue eyes of hers shone with pride, and Elizabeth was suddenly struck with an almost overpowering surge of love for the family she had sometimes taken for granted.

In the next instant the three of them lifted their Waterford crystal glasses and brought them together, less than an inch apart.

"Here's to—" Terry hesitated, then grinned "—Mike getting to the church on time."

"He'll be there," Elizabeth told her. "Harding will watch out for him."

Sally Stone shot a long, thoughtful look at her older daughter before saying, "Don't worry, Terry. Your father promised me that your groom would be at the church on time and clearheaded." Tapping her glass to the other two, she said, "Here's to my baby. May she always be as happy as she is tonight."

"Here, here," Elizabeth echoed.

"I will be," Terry whispered.

"Now go to bed," Sally said after a sip of wine.

"Mother," Terry answered with a laugh. "Ten is a little early, don't you think?"

In response, Sally took her daughter's glass and set it on the table. "I've seen the way you and Mike look at each other," she said with a knowing smile. "No doubt you'll be up all night tomorrow night. Wouldn't you like to be well rested and um…*energetic?*"

"*Mother!*" Terry laughed outright.

"What?" Sally looked at each of them. "We're all grown-ups, aren't we?"

"Apparently," Elizabeth said ruefully. It was the

first time their mother had ever talked about sex and one of her girls in the same sentence.

Terry hugged her mother tightly, gave her a resounding kiss on the forehead, then said, "You're absolutely right, Mom. I'm going to bed." She walked to the doorway, then stopped and turned around. "'Night, Lizzie," she said. "And thanks for everything."

Elizabeth took another sip of wine, letting the chilled, fruity drink slide down her throat slowly before answering. "You're welcome. I'll see you in the morning."

Terry nodded brightly and disappeared down the hallway. They heard her run up the stairs and the soft echo of a door closing.

Taking her seat beside Elizabeth again, Sally turned her wineglass between her hands. "Is everything all right, dear?"

She glanced at her mother. "Sure. Why wouldn't it be?"

"No reason," Sally said with a shrug. "It was good of you to offer to make Terry's cake."

Elizabeth smiled to herself and moved on to the next frosted layer. "I couldn't very well let her order some ordinary-looking, dry-tasting cake from a bakery, could I?"

"No, I suppose you couldn't have."

Shooting a sidelong glance at her mother, Elizabeth wondered what the woman was working up to. Her mom had never had trouble saying what was on her mind.

"I do wonder, dear," Sally said softly.

"About what?"

"Well, how you feel about your younger sister getting married before you."

"Mom," Elizabeth paused in her decorating, smoothing the pastry bag and forcing the frosting down closer to the tip. "You can't be serious."

Sally kept her gaze fixed on the wineglass between her palms. "It might bother some women, you know. Make them feel like...old maids."

Elizabeth laughed, ignoring the tiny stab of pain deep inside her. "Come on, Mom. These are the 1990s not the 1890s."

"I know that, but still, some women might have tender feelings about such a thing."

"Some women maybe. Not me."

"I hope not."

Elizabeth laid the pastry bag down and reached over to cover her mother's hand with one of hers. "Remember me, Mom? I'm the daughter who didn't *want* to get married?"

"People change."

"Not always."

"I'm not blind, Lizzie," her mother said softly.

"What's that supposed to mean?"

"I've seen the way you look at Harding Casey."

Uncomfortable with the turn the conversation had taken, Elizabeth picked up the pastry bag and went to work. It gave her a good excuse to keep from looking into her mother's eyes. Eyes that had always been able to tell truth from lies.

"Your father and I like him very much."

"Of course Dad likes him. Harding's a career Marine. What's not to like?"

"It's not just that," Sally said quickly, "though for your father, I admit it *is* a positive sign. But I think Harding is a nice man. He's polite, charming, witty and looks at you as though you're one of those desserts you're so famous for."

Heat stained her cheeks. She felt the color race up her neck, blossoming on her face like wild roses. Dipping her head closer to her work, she said, "Don't look for things that aren't there, Mom."

"I don't think I am," Sally answered quietly. Reaching for her daughter, she tipped Elizabeth's chin up with her fingertips until their gazes met and locked. "And at the same time, sweetie, don't you try to hide from something that might be the gift of a lifetime."

Tears suddenly blinded her. She didn't know whether it was her mother's gentle touch or her soft voice or the fact that those same words had been whispering around inside her own head for days. But whatever the reason, she blinked them back stubbornly.

"Harding and I are...*friends*." Somehow she just couldn't call him her lover to her mother's face. Thirty-two or not, some things one just didn't say to one's mom.

"Friends," Sally echoed sadly. "Is that all you want from him?"

"That's all there is," she said firmly.

"Lizzie honey, the sparks that fly when you two are near each other are bright enough to light up a city." She smiled tenderly. "Friends don't usually have that effect on each other."

"We're very *close* friends."

"Ahh..." Sally nodded, patted Elizabeth's cheek, then let her hand fall away. "I thought as much. It's in your eyes, honey, how much you care for him."

"Mom..."

"Does he feel the same? Yes," she answered herself in the next breath. "Of course he does. Even your dad noticed."

"Don't make this into something it isn't, Mom," Elizabeth warned her. "In three weeks Harding's being deployed to Okinawa for six months, and that will be that."

"Will it?" Sally mumbled. "I wonder."

Nine

The groomsmen, all Marines, were wearing their dress blues uniforms. Only the groom himself wore a tuxedo, and Harding was the only person who seemed to notice Mike looking at the uniforms surrounding him just a bit wistfully.

But once he had gotten a look at his bride, that expression in his eyes faded to be replaced by a joy that was so strong, Harding had had to look away from it. It was either that, or be eaten by jealousy for his best friend's good fortune.

All through the short ceremony, Harding's gaze had continually shifted to Elizabeth standing just opposite him at the small altar. Beautiful in a silvery, lilac-colored, off-the-shoulder dress, all he could think was that it should have been the two of them standing in front of the preacher. It should have been *them* repeating those ancient words about love and loyalty and commitment.

He would never have believed it of himself. But the truth was hard to ignore—especially while staring into Elizabeth's eyes.

Lifting his bottle of beer to his lips, Harding looked around the reception hall, trying to find her without seeming obvious. He took a long drink as he casually noted the other Marines in the room, each of them surrounded by a cluster of women. Smiling to himself, he remembered plenty of times when he, too, had used the effect of dress blues on civilians to his best advantage.

Odd that only a week after meeting one particular woman he had no interest in any other. Odd, or fate? he wondered. Was it really fate taking a hand in things? Had he and Elizabeth been brought together by some karmic force?

He whistled low and soft, looked at his beer bottle suspiciously, then set it down on the table beside him. Apparently two beers was enough to kick his imagination into high gear.

Fate?

Karma?

No, what had happened between them was simple science. *Chemistry.*

Across the wide, crowded hall from him, he finally caught a glimpse of the woman who had turned his brain into slush.

Busying herself around the cake table, she was making last-minute adjustments to the most-gorgeous-looking cake he had ever seen. Five layers, divided by white plastic columns, the wedding dessert had been lovingly decorated with lilac frosting flowers, silver stars and studded with real, live roses. Sterling silver rosebuds, fully bloomed lavender roses and white baby's breath, each blossom tucked into a tiny plastic bud vase then attached to the cake. Tendrils of ribbons streamed from the icing and lay in curled abandon at the base of the cake.

Elizabeth really *was* the Princess of Party Cooking.

Everyone who had seen the cake had paused to admire it. He had listened to their praise for the chef and taken great pride in every word.

"Beautiful, isn't she?" a voice from nearby asked him.

Startled out of his thoughts, Harding half turned to meet the steady gaze of Elizabeth's father. Marine Captain Harry Stone, retired, still looked as if he was ready to report to the parade ground.

At six foot one, Captain Stone stood tall and straight. A receding hairline, more gray than dark brown, and fine lines around his eyes and mouth were the only marks of age on the man.

Instinctively Harding straightened almost to attention. "Yes, sir," he said. "She is."

The captain's gaze shifted to his daughter, unaware of their regard. "You know, Lizzie always was the more hardheaded of my daughters. The one most like me, I guess."

"Sir?" Was he supposed to agree? Wouldn't that be insulting the man? Although he had to admit, Elizabeth was definitely a strong woman. One who knew her own mind and wasn't afraid to voice her opinion. It was one of the things he liked best about her.

"She's not fond of change, you know," her father was saying. "Never has been. Guess that's why she didn't like being raised in the Corps. Hated the moving. The deploying."

Harding nodded and wished for another beer. "My ex-wife felt the same way. Military marriages aren't the easiest thing in the world to maintain."

Captain Stone chuckled, shaking his head. "Never thought I'd hear a career Devil Dog complain about hard work."

Harding shot him a look. Hard work was a part of his life. He had never backed away from a challenge.

"Ease up, Sergeant Major," Elizabeth's father said softly, to avoid being overheard by the wandering guests. "I'm not trying to insult you—"

Harding nodded.

"I'm only trying to point out to you that the seemingly impossible is, most often, something we're afraid to try. Once tried, impossible becomes possible."

"Not always, Captain," Harding muttered, remembering the sense of failure he had experienced when his ex-wife left him, decrying the hard life of being married to the Corps.

"Call me Harry," the older man offered. "And no, Sergeant Major. There are no guarantees. But I can tell you from experience that a good marriage is a blessing." Unconsciously his gaze drifted from his daughter to his wife, chatting and laughing with several other women. His eyes softened, and his features gentled. "The right woman is more than a wife. She's a partner. A friend."

Harding shifted uncomfortably. What was this all about? Was the man actually trying to bring Elizabeth and him together? Hell, as her father, the captain should know better than anyone that his daughter was dead set against any kind of relationship with a career soldier.

Running one finger around the inside collar of his tunic, Harding had to wonder what this man would say if he knew that Elizabeth and he were lovers. Would he still be getting this speech about honor and commitment? Or would the captain be holding a noose?

Feeling distinctly uncomfortable with the conversation, Harding blurted, "If you'll excuse me, sir, I believe I'll go find your younger daughter and give her my condolences on marrying Mike."

The older man smiled. "Certainly, Marine. Go ahead."

Harding escaped immediately, blending into the crowd, losing himself amidst the mingle of voices, the snatches of laughter.

He didn't see the thoughtful expression on Captain Stone's face. Nor did he witness the meaningful glance the captain sent his smiling wife.

There was nothing left to do.

Elizabeth had managed to keep herself busy from the end of the ceremony until now. But she had worked herself out of a job. The buffet-style meal was being catered by a company entirely capable of managing their own help, and her masterpiece of a wedding cake was set up, awaiting its moment.

Clutching a glass of champagne, she wandered aimlessly at the edges of the crowd, smiling to friends and nodding pleasantly to strangers. Always, though, she kept one eye out for Harding.

Standing across the altar from him during the wedding, she had hardly heard the words of the ceremony. Instead, she had indulged silly daydreams—visions of Harding and her standing before a minister. Harding and her holding hands, exchanging rings and promises. Harding and her kissing before a gathering of friends and families, then listening to the applause erupt from the pews.

Silly, she told herself, and took another sip of champagne. No, more than silly. Ludicrous. She didn't even *want* to be married. Let alone to a Marine.

"Oh, Lizzie!"

She turned around in time to see her younger sister sweep down on her, veil flying, eyes sparkling. Terry enveloped her in a hug, then pulled back and grinned happily.

"Isn't this fabulous?"

"Yeah," Elizabeth said, unable to keep from returning Terry's smile. "It's wonderful."

"I actually cried at my own wedding," Terry said with a half laugh. "But it was so beautiful, I just couldn't help it."

"*You're* beautiful, kiddo."

She glanced down at her full-skirted, ivory lace wedding dress and nodded before looking back up at her sister. "You know, I think I am, today." She reached for one of Elizabeth's hands and gave it a squeeze. "The cake turned out so gorgeous. Thank you, Lizzie."

"You're welcome." Winking, she added, "And it tastes even better than it looks."

"Naturally," Terry huffed with pride.

Linking her arm through her sister's, Terry started walking slowly. "Doesn't Harding look handsome in his uniform?"

Elizabeth narrowed her gaze and looked at her sister suspiciously. Her mother had already pointed out how well Harding filled out a set of dress blues. As if she hadn't noticed without any help from her family.

Deliberately she shrugged. "I never said he wasn't handsome."

Terry's lips twitched. "Has he told you how he got his nickname? Hard Case?"

Intrigued, Elizabeth said, "No." Of course, the only time she had actually *asked* for the information, he had been otherwise occupied. A ribbon of heat swirled through her body as she recalled exactly *what* he had been doing at the time.

"Well," Terry said, apparently not noticing her sister's momentary lapse of attention. "Mike told me. It started in boot camp. Mike says Harding refused to accept less than the best from himself. He pushed himself higher and harder than any of the others—which only earned his squad mates extra duty—because he would show them up so badly."

Elizabeth nodded. That sounded like what she would have expected from Harding Casey.

"When the guys called him on it, he only challenged them to improve." Terry shook her head and smiled. "Anyway, his stubbornness started the nickname there. But when he was sent to Grenada, some of his men were pinned down by enemy fire with no way out."

Immediately Elizabeth, the daughter of a soldier, envisioned the scene in her mind. She saw a small group of Marines, trapped, with bullets biting into the dust at their feet, zinging off rocks by their heads.

Terry continued. "Apparently, when no one else could think of what to do, Harding went in, under fire, and risked his own life to pull his men out—one by one. He went back time and again until they were all safe." She shrugged, stopped and faced her sister squarely. "He simply refused to give up. Refused to accept failure."

Her eyes teared at the mental picture of Harding risking his life repeatedly for the lives of his men. It was so clear to her, she could almost hear the bullets flying.

"Lizzie," Terry whispered urgently. "There's something between you two, isn't there?"

So much for keeping it a secret, Elizabeth thought as she nodded miserably.

"I knew it," Terry crowed. "I knew you two would be good together."

"Don't book the church," Elizabeth said, before her little sister could get up a full head of steam. "Whatever Harding and I have, it's not going to end in marriage."

"Lizzie…"

"Let it go, Terry." She looked directly into her sister's eyes. "Please. You know I never planned on getting married. And Harding is shipping out in less than three weeks."

"He'll be back, though."

Yes, he would be back. But would he be coming back to her? Or would the heat of the fire between them burn itself out while he was gone?

She didn't voice her thoughts, merely shook her head sadly.

Grabbing both of her hands, Terry bent in close and whispered fiercely. "Lizzie, don't blow this. Don't blow a chance to be happy."

"Stop, Terry. You don't know—"

"I know, I know. You hate the military."

"Not the military itself," she corrected. "It's the constant moving, never belonging I don't like. And the absences. Don't you remember all of those times when Dad was gone? All of the birthdays he missed? The Christmases?"

"Sure I do," Terry said. "But I remember everything else, too. I remember his homecomings and having him there, at home every night. I remember the love."

"So do I, Terry," Elizabeth said softly, "but—"

"No buts," her sister said. "I told you how stubborn Hard Case is, right?"

Elizabeth nodded.

"If he loves you, Lizzie, he won't stop. Just like in Grenada, he'll keep coming back. He'll slip under any bullets you throw at him and keep coming back until you're convinced. As for the travel and deployment," she shrugged. "It wouldn't be hard, Lizzie. Not if you really love him."

She wanted to believe, which surprised her. A week ago she wouldn't have even entertained the notion of marriage at all. Now, here she was having a heart-to-heart with her baby sister about a Marine of all people.

Taking a deep breath, she gave her weary mind permission to shut down for a while. There was simply too much to think about. And now wasn't the time for it.

"I appreciate it, Terry," she said, leaning into her sister for a quick hug. "But Harding and I don't love each other." Not a lie, was it?

The blushing bride didn't look convinced.

"Look," Elizabeth said, "just enjoy your own wedding day, all right? Quit worrying about planning mine?"

"Okay," she finally answered. "But we'll talk about this again. When Mike and I get back from Jamaica?"

Elizabeth nodded, grateful for the respite. Hopefully, by the time the honeymooners were back, this firestorm with Harding would have fizzled out, and there would be nothing to talk about.

"There you are," Mike announced, coming up behind his new wife and swinging her in a wide circle. "No one will dance with me."

"Well," Terry retorted, "we can't have that, can we?"

As the newlyweds started for the dance floor, arm

in arm, Terry looked back over her shoulder. "Later?"

Elizabeth nodded, relieved to be alone again.

"Dance with me?" A familiar, deep voice rumbled from behind her and she slowly turned around. Her heartbeat thundered in her ears, her blood raced through her veins and her knees wobbled unsteadily.

Would she always react like this to him? she wondered. Would his voice always sink to the base of her spine and send chills coursing up and down her back?

His clear blue eyes locked with hers, and Elizabeth felt herself drowning in their depths. She couldn't have looked away if her life had hung in the balance.

"Dance with me," he repeated, this time making it a command, not a request.

She nodded slightly and took the hand he offered her. Sizzles of heat snaked up her arm from their joined hands as she followed him to the dance floor. There, he turned, pulled her into his arms and began to lead her around the floor. Swaying, their bodies touching, she let her mind wander, giving herself over to the sensation of being held by him.

Remembering that in less than three weeks he would be gone from her life.

Harding clenched his jaw tight and somehow managed to keep his grasp on her gentle. "Nice wedding," he said.

"It was, wasn't it?"

"They look happy."

She turned her head and looked at the happy couple. He did too. Mike and Terry were lost in each other. Joy radiated from them like warmth from the sun.

"What were you and your sister talking about?" he asked quietly. He had come up on them too late to overhear anything, but from the expression on Elizabeth's features, she hadn't been any too pleased with the conversation.

Elizabeth shifted her gaze to meet his. He studied those soft brown eyes for a long moment, but whatever she was thinking, she was managing to conceal it from him.

"Nothing, really," she said, and he knew she was lying.

The only reason she would have to lie was if she had been talking about him. Damn, he wondered what she had said.

"You've made quite an impression on my parents," Elizabeth said and moved with him through a slow turn.

"They're nice people." Lord, it was as if they were strangers. This polite conversation was tearing at him.

"I saw you and Dad talking together earlier," she commented.

He stiffened slightly. He wasn't about to let her know that he and his father were discussing her. She would immediately want to know what had been said—and the truth was, he wasn't very sure of that himself.

"Anything you want to tell me about?" she asked.

"No," he said, avoiding her gaze. Just like her, he was lying. Now he was convinced she and Terry had been talking about him. "Just two old Marines exchanging war stories."

She looked up at him, her eyes delving deeply into his. He would never get tired of staring into her eyes.

"My parents will be leaving tomorrow."

"So soon?" he asked, despite the fact that this seemed like the longest weekend of his life. Not being able to be with her was harder on him than boot camp had ever been.

She smiled wryly as if reading his mind. "Yes. Dad's anxious to get back to his cronies and the golf course, and Mom's sure that the volunteer staff at the local hospital can't get along without her."

Her smile didn't falter, but he could see that the thought of her parents leaving made her sad. "You'll miss them."

"Yeah, I will." Elizabeth inhaled sharply. "We don't get together often enough. But, ever since Dad retired, they're almost never home. Always off on some little trip or other."

"So even though he left the Corps, they still travel a lot."

She nodded. "I hadn't thought of it like that, but yes. Sometimes," she added wistfully, "compared to them I feel like a stick-in-the-mud."

He frowned slightly and pulled her closer against him. He inhaled the soft, sweet scent of the fresh lavender and sterling rosebuds that made up the wreath encircling her head. Harding concentrated on that scent, trying to memorize it, so that when he was alone, in Okinawa, thousands of miles from her, he would be able to draw on that memory and bring her close.

She laid her head down on his shoulder, apparently deciding to ignore whoever might be watching them. His right hand smoothed up and down her back, caressing the silk covering her flesh.

Silent now, they danced together with controlled, yet fluid movements. The intimacy of their dance announcing that they were more than polite strangers. He felt her soft sigh, and all he wanted to do was pick her up, carry her to the Mustang outside and drive like a shot to her condo.

But he couldn't. Not with her parents in residence.

Memories of the past few days filled him, making his body tight and hard and filling his mind with erotic images of Elizabeth.

He saw her as he made love to her, looking into her eyes as a climax took her. He saw her smile and reach for him. He saw her naked in her kitchen, scrambling eggs for the two of them at one in the morning.

His right hand slipped lower on her back, riding just above the swell of her behind. His fingers itched to touch her. The crowd of dancers swirled around them, but for him, it was as if they were alone in the room. All he saw was her. All he felt was her.

All he wanted was her.

A warning jolt shot through him. For all of his care, all of his noble intentions of keeping his distance, he wanted Elizabeth. Not just for the few short weeks he had remaining stateside, but for a lifetime.

But a lifetime of Elizabeth meant marriage.

The truth shocked him.

The depths of his feelings rattled around inside him like a sword in a scabbard.

He loved her. More than he had ever imagined it possible to love a woman, he loved Elizabeth Stone.

Yet that simple fact was met and challenged by another.

She didn't want a husband. And even if she did, he had already tried marriage...and failed miserably.

Ten

Two weeks slipped by with almost eerie speed.

Elizabeth tried not to notice the calendar. She made every effort to not think beyond the moment. Daily, while working in her kitchen, testing new recipes, she had to focus to keep her mind on the work at hand. And still her gaze drifted to the clock on the wall, slowly counting down the hours until Harding would arrive.

She turned the water on, sending clouds of steam rushing up into her face. Squirting liquid soap into the sink, she absently watched bubbles froth and blossom on the surface of the wash water. Somewhere in the back of her mind, she noticed that the Beethoven CD had ended, but she didn't move to replace it. Instead, as she picked up a dishcloth and began to work, she indulged herself in thoughts of Harding.

They had eased into a familiar routine over the past two weeks. He reported for duty at the base every morning, then as soon as his shift was finished, he drove to her condo. They had dinner, rented movies and sometimes went for walks on the beach.

And they loved.

Elizabeth shivered as she washed a cherished ceramic bowl and set it in the dish drainer. She rarely used the dishwasher, since most of her equipment was too treasured to trust to machinery. Besides, washing dishes freed her mind, and she had thought up some of her best recipes while her hands were buried in soapsuds.

As she turned off the water, she reached for a fresh towel and began drying the mountain of mixing bowls and utensils. While she worked, her mind wandered back to the subject that seemed to fascinate it most.

Harding Casey.

Images raced through her brain. Erotic images. Loving images. Together they had christened nearly every room in her condo. There wasn't a place in her home where she could go and not be reminded of him. His touch. His kisses. His deep voice and the whispered words of passion that had been ingrained in her memory.

All night, every night, they lay in each other's arms, talking of their pasts, because any mention of a future would only destroy their present. And every morning at dawn he rose from her bed, showered and dressed. Then he left her to return to the base.

And every morning when he was gone, she moved over on her queen-size mattress to lie where he had lain. The still-warm sheets comforted her, his pillow rested beneath her head, and she dreamed of that night, when he would come again.

But the few short days they had left were quickly passing. In no time she would be alone again.

What would she do when he was gone?

Mechanically she walked around the kitchen, returning her equipment to its proper places. Soon, he would be leaving. Six long months when she wouldn't see him…be held by him.

And there was no guarantee that she would see him again when he returned, either. She stopped short, caught by that thought. Did she *want* a guarantee? Wasn't she the one who had insisted from the start that she wasn't looking for a long-term relationship? Hadn't she insisted that marriage wasn't in her plans?

Marriage? Where had that come from?

She almost laughed aloud at the pitiful attempt at self-delusion. Thoughts of marriage had been lurking near the edge of her consciousness for days. So far she hadn't let them get any further.

Tossing the damp towel down onto the butcher-block counter, Elizabeth stared around at the world she'd created for herself so painstakingly. Up-to-the-minute appliances. Plenty of workspace. Homey, yet modern. Everything she had wanted her home to be.

And yet…until meeting Harding Casey, she had never noticed just how *empty* it was. How the wind blowing across the shutters sounded like a soft sigh. Folding her arms over her chest, she leaned against the countertop, feeling the edge of the butcher block bite into the base of her spine.

Had the place *always* been this quiet? she wondered. Was that the reason she was constantly feeding the CD player or flipping on the TV? Or had she noticed the quiet now merely because the past three weeks she had rarely been alone?

Rubbing her face briskly with both hands, she then reached up and yanked her tortoiseshell headband off. Instantly a budding headache eased. She combed her fingers through her hair and tugged at the hem of her pale pink tank top.

Glancing down at herself, she wondered vaguely if she should change clothes before Harding arrived. A white splotch of flour and water had crusted over, in the center of her shirt between her breasts, and there was a grease stain on the right leg of her cutoff denim shorts.

Then she heard the front door open.

"Elizabeth?"

"In here," she called out, a familiar excitement already flooding her system. Her stomach muscles tightened, and every inch of her body went on red alert. Would she always feel this incredible surge of elation just at the sound of his voice?

He stepped through the kitchen doorway, a white paper bag resting in the curve of one arm. A familiar, somehow cloying, aroma filled the kitchen and Elizabeth swallowed heavily.

"Chinese?" she asked.

He shrugged and set the bag on the table. "I figured you might like takeout for a change."

Thoughtful. She loved Chinese food. Her stomach jumped again, but this time it wasn't as pleasant a sensation. Licking suddenly dry lips, she tried to ignore the flutter of unease rippling through her.

"Getting tired of my cooking?" she teased as she took a step closer to him.

"Nope," he assured her with a wink. "But I've got plans for you lady…and they don't include cooking."

Oh, Lord. Her knees turned to jelly, and damp heat rushed to her center. "What kind of plans?" she asked, after clearing her throat.

He pulled her up tight against him and wrapped his arms around her. Elizabeth closed her eyes tight, wanting to always remember what it felt like to be held this close to him. There were six months of lonely nights ahead of her, and she would need every one of her memories to survive them.

She bent her head and buried her nose in his shoulder, hoping to avoid the almost overpowering odor of sweet-and-sour sauce.

Harding threaded his fingers through her hair, cupping the back of her head in his palm.

The need didn't ease. The hunger he felt for her only strengthened with each passing day. He kept telling himself that a passion as hot as theirs couldn't last. Couldn't sustain itself. But not only did it continue to burn, it continued to surpass itself.

She shuddered in his arms, and he told himself he was a lucky man. There weren't many men, he would wager, who had a woman as eager for him as he was for her. Smiling to himself, he looked down and eased her head back until he could see her clearly.

Eyes closed, her lips clamped tightly, she looked a

bit paler than she had when he had walked in. As he watched her, she swallowed heavily, inhaled, then grimaced.

"Elizabeth?" he asked, sudden concern overriding his desire. "Are you all right?"

"I'm fine," she said through clenched teeth.

"Well, you don't *look* fine," he told her. As he spoke he saw tiny beads of sweat break out on her forehead. Alarmed, he laid the back of his hand against her clammy skin to check for a fever.

She pushed back out of his arms. "I'm not sick, Harding," she said, her voice ringing with determination. "It's just that smell."

Frowning, he studied her. "What smell?"

Elizabeth waved one hand at the sack on the table. "That." She inhaled sharply again, scowled and took a few steps away from the food. "Can't you smell it?"

He sniffed the air appreciatively. "Yeah. It smells great."

She shook her head, lifting one hand to cover her mouth. "What did you get, anyway?"

"Your favorites," he said, really confused now. "Egg rolls, fried rice, cashew chicken and sweet-and-sour pork."

"That's the smell." Her lips pulled back from her teeth, and she nearly snarled at the cartoned food.

"What?" He reached into the sack, pulling out one of the small white cartons. "The pork?" he asked, opening the top and taking a step toward her. "It's the same stuff we had last week. You loved it."

She backed up like a vampire from a cross. "No.

It's different. The sweet-and-sour sauce. Must be bad.''

He inhaled deeply, letting the mingle of spices and seasonings rush into his lungs. Nothing wrong there, he told himself, and glanced at the woman still back-pedaling out of the kitchen. If he wasn't mistaken, Elizabeth's features had taken on a decidedly green cast.

"Are you all right?"

"Yes," she said quickly, then shook her head. Her eyes wide, she mumbled, "No," just before she turned and ran out of the room.

Hot on her heels, Harding rounded the corner to the bathroom in time to hold her head as she was thoroughly sick. Several minutes later he offered her a damp washcloth and led her to the living room. There, he sat her on the couch and eased down onto the coffee table directly opposite her.

"How long have you been sick?" he asked. He didn't want to think about her lying around the house all day, miserable and alone.

"I wasn't sick," she said. "Not until I got a whiff of that…" she shuddered and pointed at the kitchen.

"You mean the—"

She held one hand up. "Please. Don't even say it."

Reaching out, he touched her forehead again, pleased to note that she didn't seem quite so chilled and clammy anymore. "No fever."

Letting her head fall against the overstuffed sofa back, she muttered thickly, "I told you. I'm not sick."

"Then why else would you—" He stopped dead.

As far as he knew there was only one reason—other than the flu or food poisoning—for a woman to be sick to her stomach.

The same thought had apparently occurred to her. She lifted her head gingerly and looked at him. "This doesn't necessarily mean a thing."

"Yeah, right." He stood up, keeping his gaze locked with hers. "When were you due?"

"Excuse me?"

"Stow it, princess," he said softly. "When?"

"A few days ago." When he jerked her a nod and started for the front door, she added quickly, "But I've been late before."

"I'll be right back," he told her as he grabbed the doorknob and turned.

"Where are you going?" she asked.

"To the drugstore," he said simply. "It's time to find out one way or the other."

He actually purchased two different pregnancy test kits. Elizabeth stared at Harding as he paced aimlessly around her bedroom. When he returned from the pharmacy with the kits, he had told her that they shouldn't trust such a major test to one kit. She couldn't help wondering though if the real reason was he was hoping for two different responses so they could have another bit of breathing space.

Elizabeth didn't know *what* she was hoping for.

She'd gone over and over the options in her mind, but none of the other choices were valid ones for *her*. She couldn't give away her own child, only to perhaps have to one day face an eighteen-year-old adult angry about being abandoned. As for the other choice, she couldn't reconcile herself to that idea at all.

"Isn't it time, yet?" Harding asked.

She glanced over at him and sympathized. His solemn, almost-grim features echoed her own.

"No," she said. "The timer's set. It'll ring when the tests are finished."

He nodded, rubbed one hand over the back of his neck and stared down at the rose-colored carpet. "Five minutes never seemed so long before."

"I know." She wished time could stand still. She wished she could think of something brilliant—or comforting—to say.

A digital timer screeched suddenly, sending both of them into a dash for the doorway. Elizabeth beat him since she was a good three feet closer. Shutting off the ringing alarm, she took a deep breath, picked up the two plastic wands and looked down into the test squares.

"Well?" Harding asked from behind her. "What's the verdict?"

Her hands trembling, she inhaled sharply and forced a smile as she turned around to face him. "The verdict is mixed," she said.

"What do you mean?" He took a step closer. "One says yes, the other no?"

"Not quite," she told him as a wave of uneasiness washed over her. "According to these, I'm definitely pregnant."

Not a flicker of emotion showed on his face. "Then what's this 'mixed verdict' business about?"

"Well." She choked on a laugh. "One's pink, the

other's blue. So I'm pregnant, we just don't know what it is, a boy or a girl.''

"That's not very funny." If anything, his features had become even more solemn.

"Give me a minute, I'm new at this." She was babbling. She could feel it. She just couldn't stop it. "I know, it's twins. A boy *and* a girl."

"Elizabeth…"

"Or, no." She waved both wands in the air like a drunken conductor. "I know—with our luck, it's quadruplets!"

Harding stepped up close to her. Taking the test sticks from her hands, he glanced at the results, then laid them both down on the counter behind her.

Elizabeth shivered, suddenly cold right down to her bones. She was talking a mile a minute and he was too damned quiet.

A baby.

At thirty-two years old, she was going to have a baby.

A sheen of tears filled her eyes, and her vision blurred. Dropping one hand to her flat abdomen, she laid her palm gently atop her nesting child as if to apologize for ever wishing it away.

Harding saw the movement and immediately covered her hand with his. She looked up at him, and he was struck to the core by the unexpected film of tears shimmering in her eyes.

"Good heavens, Harding," she whispered, her voice catching on a strangled sob. "We actually made a baby."

His throat too tight to speak, he simply pulled her

into the circle of his arms. Nestling her head beneath his chin, he gently stroked her back with long, caressing movements in an attempt to calm and comfort her.

A baby.

At thirty-eight he was going to be a father.

Something inside his chest tightened around his heart until he thought that organ might burst. Most of his life, he'd been alone. He hadn't had a family since he was a kid. And except for his one glaring failure at marriage, he had never *tried* to create a family of his own.

The Corps had always been enough.

Until now.

"I suppose," she said, her voice muffled against his chest, "you want to talk about it right this minute."

He smiled briefly. She knew him well. "Yeah," he said, dropping a kiss onto the top of her head. "I do."

She pulled in one long, shuddering breath and nodded before stepping away from him. "Okay, but let's go into the kitchen, huh? I could use some coffee."

He frowned as she stepped past him and made her way down the hall. "Do you think you should be drinking caffeine?"

"Oh." Elizabeth's steps faltered slightly. "I don't know. I guess not, though. Okay, I'll settle for herbal tea."

Following after her, he took a seat at the kitchen table and waited for her to settle herself. Strange, how well he had gotten to know her in the past three weeks. He knew that she needed to be moving when her mind was busy. He also knew that until she sat down with her cup of tea in hand, she wasn't going to be listening to him.

As she moved around the room, he let his mind drift. In less than a week, he would be shipping out for Okinawa. He wouldn't be here to help her through the next several months. He wouldn't be able to hold her head for her when she was sick or to comfort her when she was worried.

Harding leaned back in his chair and reached up to undo his collar button and yank his tie off. She sat down on the opposite side of the table, cupped her mug between her palms and took a long, slow sip of tea. Only then did she look at him.

"You haven't said much," she accused gently.

That was only one of the differences between them, he thought. When her emotions ran high, so did her tongue. He, on the other hand, had a tendency to keep quiet until he had his thoughts together.

"I want to make sure I say what I have to say right."

Her gaze flicked away from his, then back again. She looked to be steeling herself. "What do you have to say, Harding? Just spit it out. Lord knows, I did."

"All right," he said. Reaching across the table separating them, he took her mug and set it aside. Then he covered both of her hands with his. There was really only one thing to say, and he had to get it right. Everything depended on it. Inhaling sharply, deeply, he said on a rush, "I want you to marry me before I ship out, Elizabeth."

She drew her hands out from under his. Staring

straight into his eyes, she said softly, "Somehow, I knew that's what you were going to say."

"That's not an answer," he reminded her.

"You're right," she agreed and nodded absently. "But this is. My answer is no, Harding. I *won't* marry you. I can't."

Eleven

"**W**hy the hell not?"

She winced inwardly. That short, sharp question came out in a voice rough with undisguised frustration. Elizabeth could understand how he felt, and she really didn't enjoy turning down a marriage proposal from the father of her newly discovered child. But she wasn't about to sacrifice the lives of three people on the altar of *propriety*.

Preparing herself for what she knew would be a fierce battle, she deliberately kept her voice even and calm as she said, "Because you don't love me, Harding. You're proposing for the wrong reason."

He jumped to his feet, sending his chair clattering to the floor. Stopping, he bent, righted the chair again, then strode to the sink where he turned around to look at her again. "How do you know I *don't* love you?

Maybe I've loved you all along and was too stupid— or too wary to say so."

Something inside her leaped at that notion, and she deliberately quashed the budding eagerness. She knew Harding Casey well. He was an honorable man to whom doing the right thing came as second nature. Of course he would lie and proclaim his love. He didn't want to ship out on deployment leaving behind his pregnant lover without *trying* to help.

"No, Harding," she said firmly. "You never would have asked me to marry you if I weren't pregnant."

"We'll never know that for sure, will we?"

No, they wouldn't. A small spear of regret shivered through her. How strange life was, she told herself. A month ago she would have sworn that she wasn't the slightest bit interested in marriage. She had long since buried her old dreams of children and resigned herself to the knowledge that she would never be a mother.

Now, four weeks later, she was pregnant and refusing the proposal of a man she loved.

Love. She breathed slowly, deeply as the acknowledgment settled into her bones. She loved Harding Casey. Career Marine. That elusive emotion had sneaked up on her when she wasn't looking, and now things were too complicated for her to surrender to a love that might be all one-sided.

"You wouldn't have proposed, Harding," she insisted. He'd made it perfectly clear from the beginning of their relationship that he wasn't looking for a wife, any more than she wanted a husband.

"Oh," he said, slipping into sarcasm, "so now you're the *Psychic* Princess of Party Cooking?"

"You said yourself that you had already tried marriage once and weren't interested in trying again."

"That was then. Things are different now."

She nodded sadly. "I know. The baby."

He inhaled sharply and curled his fingers tightly around the edge of the countertop. "Yes, the baby. This changes things. But dammit, Elizabeth, I cared about you before the baby, and you know it."

"Caring and wanting to marry someone are two entirely different things." Elizabeth folded her hands in her lap and tried to rein in her rising temper. "There's no reason for us to fight about this, Harding."

"There's plenty of reason, princess," he countered and crossed her kitchen floor in a few long, angry strides. Glaring down at her, he went on. "In less than a week, I'm out of here. I'll be thousands of miles away for six damn months."

"Harding," she tried to interrupt.

"And you'll be here, pregnant with *my* baby. Alone."

She stood up, folded her arms across her chest and met his glare with one of her own. "I've lived alone for quite a while now, you know. I've managed to take care of myself quite nicely so far without the help of a certain Sergeant Major."

"Yeah, well up to now you haven't been pregnant, have you?"

No, she hadn't. A momentary thread of worry unwound within her. Oh, she didn't doubt that she could handle the pregnancy on her own. But once the baby was here, then what?

She paused mentally and almost sighed in relief. Apparently she had already made the most important decision. There would *definitely* be a baby.

Already Elizabeth felt the first stirrings of a long-denied maternal urge. She could no more rid herself of this baby than she could stop breathing. But answering one question only posed more.

What would her fairly liberal parents have to say about their unmarried, oldest daughter giving birth to their first grandchild? Could she handle the incredible responsibility of raising a child? And most important, was she capable of giving a child enough love so that it wouldn't miss having a live-in father? Or would she louse things up so badly her child would one day tell a doctor that "it's all my mother's fault"?

"Elizabeth?"

She dismissed her wandering thoughts and focused her attention on the man standing so close to her. "I'm sorry, Harding."

He grabbed her upper arms and pulled her closer. Staring into her eyes, looking for reassurance, he asked, "Are you going to—"

"No," she said. "I'm not going to end the pregnancy."

He exhaled heavily, clearly relieved.

"In fact," she said and forced a half smile. "I want to thank you."

"For what?"

"For the baby."

Harding shook his head briskly as if he couldn't believe what he was hearing. "Thank me?"

"Yes. I had given up on the hope of having children. So thank you."

"Oh." He released her and took a long step back. "You're welcome. Anytime."

She stiffened slightly, and Harding was sure his sarcastic comment had struck home. Dammit, she was shutting him out as completely as if he had already left the country. He felt like a sperm donor. Thanks so much, goodbye now. Have a nice life. Well, she wasn't going to get rid of him so easily.

Reaching up, he smoothed both hands along the sides of his head. How was he supposed to convince her to marry him if he couldn't convince her that he loved her?

Blast it, he should have said something at the wedding. Or any time during the past two weeks. Why hadn't he asked her to marry him sooner? Before the baby. Hell, he knew why. Because he'd been a husband once before...and done a poor job of it, too. He hadn't wanted to risk hurting Elizabeth *or* himself with another failure.

Even now the thought of marriage terrified him. But the thought of living without her paralyzed him. And now there was his child to consider, too. His child. A well of emotion rose up in his chest. He wanted to be a part of his kid's life. Not a part-time parent every other weekend and three weeks in the summer.

He wanted it all. A home. Elizabeth. The baby. But even if she believed he loved her, would she marry him? Or would his being in the Corps stand in their way? What would he do then? Was he willing to give up his career? The only life he'd ever known? The Corps was more than a job to him. It was his life. It was a matter of pride. And honor. And duty. Could he stop being a Marine? Even if it meant having Elizabeth?

"You want me to resign, Elizabeth?" he asked suddenly, steeling himself for her answer.

She took a step toward him. "I would never ask you to give up who you are for me."

"You hate the military."

"I hate the absences. The moving around."

"That's part of it."

"I know," she said. "But, Harding, your leaving the Corps wouldn't change the fact that you proposed for the sake of your child."

"I didn't, though," he retorted, and reached for her again. He felt her tremble beneath his hands and lowered his voice. "I love you. Dammit, I never thought I'd be saying those words, Elizabeth. But I am, and I mean them."

"Harding," she started.

"No." He pulled her tightly to him, wrapping his arms around her and holding on for dear life. "I *love* you." Staring down into her soft brown eyes, he willed her to read the truth in his. But all he saw shining up at him was a deep sadness. "You're a hardheaded woman, Elizabeth, but I don't give up easily."

"You should, Harding," she said. "For both our sakes."

"I can't," he told her solemnly. "For that very reason."

She laid her palms against his chest and pushed out of his arms. The ache inside him blossomed as she tried to distance herself from him. He saw her close herself off as effectively as if she had stepped into a tiny room and shut the door behind her.

"Elizabeth," he said softly, already feeling her loss. "I won't be pushed away. Not from you and not from my child."

She threw a quick glance at him. "I would never try to keep you from your child."

"You are. Now."

"No, I'm just refusing to marry you."

"It's the same thing."

"No, it isn't," she replied hotly. "Lots of people share custody of their children. The kids grow up fine."

"Most do," he admitted. It was all slipping away from him. He felt it go and was powerless to stop it. "But if those kids had a choice, I figure most of them would want their mom and dad living in the same house. They'd rather be together."

"Sometimes we don't get a choice."

"And sometimes we do—we just make the wrong one," he countered quickly. "Don't do that, Elizabeth. Don't make a choice we'll all be sorry for. I don't want to be a visitor in my kid's life." He paused a moment, then added, "Or yours."

Her bottom lip trembled slightly, but she lifted her chin and fought through whatever she was feeling. "This will all work out, Harding. You'll see."

"All I see is that you're willing to turn your back on me and what we've found together."

She crossed her arms over her chest and rubbed her hands up and down her arms. "What we found was just what we both wanted, Harding. A few weeks together. A temporary affair enjoyed by two adults."

And they called *him* Hard Case. Stepping up close to her, he cupped her face in his hands and held her still when she would have moved away. "That's how it started, princess. I don't deny that we weren't *looking* for love. But whether we wanted it or not, it's here."

She shook her head and closed her eyes against his piercing gaze.

"It's here, princess. And it's the real thing. I think it always was, despite what we told ourselves. Trust me on this. I know." He smiled sadly, remembering the one other time in his life when he had thought himself in love. That puny emotion wasn't a tenth of what he had found with Elizabeth. Damn, why hadn't he had the courage to face that one simple fact before now? When he might have had a chance. "If we throw it away, not only will we miss an opportunity to be happy...our baby will be cheated out of a family."

"Stop, Harding," she whispered, still keeping her eyes closed. "Please stop."

"I'll never stop, Elizabeth." He stroked her cheekbones with the pads of his thumbs, wiping away a solitary tear that had seeped from the corner of her eye. "I don't quit. Even when it might be less painful to walk away, I don't." He bent his head and planted a series of soft, gentle kisses along her brow. "You can't get rid of me, and the only way you can convince me to stop asking you to marry me is to tell me you don't love me."

She opened her mouth to speak, and he had to smile at her stubbornness. Covering her lips with his fingertips, he added, "Say it and *mean* it."

She closed her mouth and opened her eyes. He was heartened to see a sheen of tears filming over their deep brown color. She loved him. She was simply too afraid to take a chance. He understood fear. But cowering in a corner trying to avoid it only made fear a stronger, more terrifying opponent. He had to make her see that the only way to defeat the fear was to stand against it.

Together. "This isn't over," he whispered. "Not by a long shot."

Two days later Elizabeth stared at her most recent culinary disaster.

"Why did no one ever tell me that pregnant women can't bake?" she muttered. Grabbing her cow-shaped hot pads, she picked up the torte pan and carried it to the trash can. There she dumped the charred pastry and glared in disgust at the mess.

It wasn't being pregnant that was ruining her ability to cook. It was thoughts of Harding. Blast him, she hadn't been able to think about anything but him since he'd left her house two nights before.

And the situation wasn't being helped by the fact that she hadn't heard so much as a word from him in that time, either. What happened to all of his talk about not quitting? Not giving up on her? Was this some bizarre backward way of asking a woman to marry you? By ignoring her until she lost her mind, then sweeping in and overpowering her?

Setting the still-hot pan onto a folded-up, blue-checked towel, she plopped down into a chair. Resting her elbow on the tabletop, she propped her chin on her knuckles and glanced at the clock on the opposite wall.

Only one in the afternoon. She still had way too much daylight left before she could go to bed. Not that she could even look forward to sleep these days. Her dreams were filled with Harding, and memories of the past few weeks. The images tore at her, preventing sleep. Last night she had even dreamed about her child—only her unborn baby had been about six in her dream. Six and angry. Angry that his daddy wasn't around and furious that she wasn't doing anything about it.

Elizabeth yawned, then frowned when the phone rang, interrupting her perfectly good self-pity party.

Pushing herself to her feet, she walked across the room, leaned her back against the wall and snatched the receiver from its cradle.

"Yes?"

"Elizabeth Stone?" a deep voice asked.

A ridiculous flutter of excitement rippled through her body before she realized that the voice was unfamiliar.

"Yes? Who is this?" She straightened up from the wall.

"This is Captain Haynes at Camp Pendleton."

Dread settled in her chest. Her stomach took a nosedive, and she had to swallow past a hard knot in her throat. Danger to a soldier didn't solely exist on a battlefield. There were training accidents all the time. Her heartbeat unsteady, she forced herself to ask, "What is it? Is Harding all right? Was he hurt?"

"No, ma'am, the Sergeant Major is fine," the voice said. "In fact, I'm actually calling on his behalf."

Relief rushed in to replace the dread. "What do you mean?"

"I'd like to offer myself as a character witness for Sergeant Major Casey," the captain said.

"I'm sorry?" She frowned at the phone in her hand.

"I've known Sergeant Major Casey for several years now. I find him to be an exemplary Marine and an honorable man."

Elizabeth crossed the room to the sink, stretching out the phone cord to its limits. Turning on the tap, she poured herself a glass of cold water, took a quick sip and said, "That's very nice to hear, Captain. But I don't understand why you would call me to—"

"I owe Harding Casey," the man said, effectively cutting her off. "If I can help him straighten things out with his fiancée, I'm happy to help."

She inhaled sharply, set the glass down and walked back to the phone cradle. Fiancée. Varied emotions scattered through her like fallen leaves caught in a whirlwind. Amusement, anger, frustration, sympathy and love all warred within her, battling for supremacy. Finally she gathered her wits and told him very politely, "I appreciate your thoughtfulness, Captain."

She wasn't going to tell the man that she wasn't engaged to Harding. It would be the same as calling him a liar, and that she wasn't prepared to do. Especially to his commanding officer.

"Not a problem at all, Ms. Stone," he said, and his voice sounded as though he was pleased with the results of his call. "If there's anything else I can do, please feel free to contact me here at the base."

"Thank you," she managed to say, "but I think you've done enough."

After he hung up, Elizabeth slammed the phone back into its base and glared at it. What was Harding up to now? Was he going to have every officer he knew call her to vouch for him? Did he really think that other people's opinions would be enough to sway her decision?

She shook her head and wished there were more time. More time for Harding and her to know each other. To get used to the idea of a baby. But she was out of time and she knew it. In just a few more days he would be leaving.

The doorbell rang and she jumped, startled. Tossing a glance from the now-silent phone to the front door, she wondered briefly if she should even answer the thing. For all she knew, the Marine Corps marching band might be standing in her front yard.

She laughed at her own exaggeration, determinedly went to the front door and threw it open wide. On her porch stood two women about her age, a blonde and a brunette, each of them with a toddler by the hand. "Can I help you?" she asked hesitantly.

"Are you Elizabeth Stone?" one of the women asked.

Wary now, she answered slowly. "Yeesss…"

They smiled at her. "Thank goodness," the blonde said. "We've been driving around this condominium complex for twenty minutes. They all look alike!"

Foolishly Elizabeth felt she should apologize for their troubles. She didn't. "Do I know you?"

"Nope," the brunette assured her as she picked up her little girl who'd begun to whine and slung her on one hip. "We're here because of Hard Case."

A sinking sensation started in the middle of her chest and slowly drifted down her body until it came to rest in the pit of her stomach. Apparently Harding wasn't finished "convincing" her yet.

"Let me guess," she said wryly. "Character witnesses?"

"Heck, no," the blonde replied. "Harding doesn't need a character witness. Anyone who knows him will tell you that."

The brunette spoke up, her voice drowning out her friend's defensive, squeaky tone. "Harding told us you were engaged, but that you were a little leery about marrying into the Corps."

Perfect. She swallowed back a groan of frustration. These women weren't at fault. This was all Harding's doing.

"He thought it might help if we talked to you," the brunette finished.

Trapped, Elizabeth's good manners kicked in. Her mother would have been proud. "Would you like to come in?"

"No, thanks," the blonde said as she bent to scoop up her son. "Tony's tired and we want to get back home for nap time. We only stopped by because we were up here shopping and—"

"It doesn't matter why we stopped," the brunette cut in again. "We only wanted to tell you that we can understand how you feel." She glanced at her friend. "Neither one of us was real crazy about marrying a Marine, either."

"Yeah," the blonde said. "I never figured me to be the military type." She shrugged and smiled. "But you can't plan who you'll fall in love with. Besides, it worked out fine." She grinned at her friend, then looked back at Elizabeth. "For both of us."

"Marines aren't always the easiest men to live with," the brunette continued as she gently pressed her daughter's head into her shoulder where the child promptly fell asleep. "But they are definitely the best."

Elizabeth felt she should say *something* in her own defense, so she blurted, "My father is a retired captain. I know about life in the Corps."

Rather than getting approval from one Marine family to another, she received a frosty glare from the brunette.

"If you're Marine, what's the problem? You should already know what life in the Corps is like."

"I *do* know. That's the problem." She couldn't believe she was having such a conversation with strangers! Just wait until she saw Harding Casey again. "Look, I've done my share of suitcase living.

It's not something I enjoy. Surely you can understand that.''

The blonde shook her head slowly as if sorry for Elizabeth. The brunette was a tad more direct. "My husband risks his *life* for his country," she said solemnly, yet with a spark of defiance. "All he asks of me is that I risk moving to a new neighborhood every few years.''

Elizabeth hadn't really thought of it like that, and she felt slightly ashamed of herself. Her lifelong complaint sounded suddenly petty and childish. Still, she had to ask. "What about your kids? Don't you worry about dragging them all over the world?''

"My kids will see places most children won't,'' the brunette told her. "And they'll be proud that their daddy served his country.'' Half turning to her friend, she said quietly, "Come on, Sharon. We better get the kids home.''

The blonde smiled a goodbye, then started for their car. The brunette stayed a minute longer.

"My husband is a Staff Sergeant,'' she said. "We've known Harding Casey off and on for years. They don't come any better than him.''

"I know,'' Elizabeth whispered and felt the truth of that statement down to her soul. If she could only be sure of his love. But she couldn't. If she surrendered to her own fears of being a single mother and married him now, she would never know if he had proposed because he loved her—or because of the baby.

The brunette stared at her for a long minute and apparently approved of what she saw. When she finally nodded, she smiled and said, "Good. If you know that much, any problem can be worked out." She stepped off the porch and onto the walk.

Elizabeth opened the door and called out, "Hey, I don't even know your name."

Stopping, the brunette turned around and grinned. "Sorry. I'm Tess Macguire." She jerked her head toward the car. "That's Sharon Trask." In a lower voice she added, "Her husband's still a corporal, but he's up for promotion."

"Thanks for stopping by," Elizabeth said automatically. Her manners were really excellent, she thought, as she realized she had just thanked two strangers for butting into her life.

The two women waved as their car pulled out from the curb. Before the sound of their engine had died away, a florist's van came to a stop in front of her house. As she watched, a young man leaped out of the van, walked around to the back and opened the doors. He reached inside and came back out with the biggest bouquet Elizabeth had ever seen.

Roses. Roses of every color and scent. Packed tightly together and tied with a pale blue ribbon attached to a mylar balloon that read Marry Me in bright red letters.

Dumbfounded, she took the flowers from the delivery boy, snatched a small white envelope from the cluster of blossoms and opened it. As the van drove off, her gaze scanned the brief message. "Elizabeth, I love you. Marry me. Harding."

She inhaled sharply, unwittingly drawing the mingled scents of the roses deep inside her lungs. Biting her lip, she clutched the bouquet tightly and stepped back inside the house. She hurriedly closed the door on the world, just in case a general happened by.

When the phone rang again, she wasn't even surprised.

It had to be Harding. Unwilling to set the flowers down, she held them to her chest and snatched up the cordless phone closest to her.

Before she could even say hello, she heard her mother's voice demand, "Why didn't you tell us you were getting married?"

Twelve

She spent nearly a half hour soothing her mother and assuring her that she would be invited to the wedding—if there ever was one. Thank God Harding had had the sense not to mention the baby when he had made his call. But no sooner had she hung up with her mother than the phone rang again. Elizabeth spent the next hour fielding phone calls from everyone Harding Casey had ever known.

Finally, in desperation, she took the phone off the hook.

With her drapes drawn, door closed and locked, the phone beeping and metallically cursing at her, Elizabeth plopped down onto the couch. She felt like a prisoner in her own home. She was being outflanked by a professional soldier and didn't have the slightest idea how to fight back.

Turning her head, she glanced at the lead crystal vase, sitting in the center of the coffee table. She glared at the bouquet of roses and told herself she should throw them out or, better yet, send them back. But it was too late for the latter, and she couldn't quite bring herself to toss them into the trash.

She felt as though she was being bombarded from all sides. She couldn't think straight anymore. All she was sure of was that she couldn't afford to surrender to Harding's campaign. If she made a mistake, her baby would have to pay the price. And that, she wasn't willing to risk.

The doorbell rang, and her gaze shot to the closed door.

A moment later three brisk knocks sounded in the stillness. What now? she wondered. A parade? Groaning slightly, she pushed up from the couch and walked quietly to the door. There, she peered through the peephole and saw a thoroughly bored-looking teenage girl clutching a clipboard of all things. Looking past the gum-chewing redhead, Elizabeth studied her empty yard as if expecting an assault team to leap up from behind the rows of pansies and storm her house. A long minute passed before she decided the coast was clear.

She opened the door, faced the girl and asked, "Yes?"

"You Elizabeth Stone?" The redhead squinted at her.

Though she was beginning to seriously consider changing her name, she had to say, "Yes, I am. What is it?"

The teenager held up the clipboard and gave it a wave. "Got a telegram for you." She unhooked a small, yellow envelope, then held out the clipboard toward Elizabeth. "Gotta sign for it."

Sighing, Elizabeth edged the screen door open, scrawled her name across line nineteen, then took the envelope.

"You should get your phone checked, lady," the girl said. "They tried to call the telegram in, but something's wrong with the line."

"Thanks," she said, having no intention of putting that phone back on the hook. She reached for her purse, lying on the entry table. Grabbing for her wallet, she pulled a dollar bill free and handed it to the girl.

"Hey, thanks, lady," the teenager said with a grin.

Elizabeth nodded absently, then stepped back and closed the door. Leaning against it, she tore open the envelope and read the all-too-brief message inside. "Six o'clock tonight. Be ready. We have to talk. Harding."

Unbelievable.

She stared at the telegram a moment longer, then slowly, completely, crumpled it in one fist. He ignores her for two days, tells everyone he knows that they're engaged and sends them to plead his case for him, then has the nerve to order her around? Elizabeth pushed away from the door, stalked her way to the kitchen and unceremoniously tossed his precious telegram into the trash can. Who did he think he was, anyway? The man had even had the nerve to lie to *her* parents about them.

"Oh," she said with a tight smile, "I'll be ready, Harding Casey. I only hope you are."

Harding watched the limousine pull up and park. He tugged at the hem of his dress blue tunic and tried to ignore the rush of nerves sweeping through him. Hell, he'd been in battle. He'd crawled to safety under withering enemy fire.

Why was it that facing this one woman could bring him to his knees?

Because, he told himself, the object of war was to simply stay alive. To keep existing. The object of this crusade with Elizabeth was *life*. Not just existing. But really and truly living for the first time. If he lost this skirmish, he'd have nothing.

The limo driver opened the back door, and she stepped out. Just looking at her took his breath away. She straightened up, smoothed her black skirt and glanced around for a minute before she saw him. Then her eyes widened and her jaw dropped visibly.

Good. He'd gone to a lot of trouble to ensure just that reaction. As she looked around, he followed her gaze, seeing it through her eyes.

Alongside one of the fire rings set up for barbecues at the Huntington Beach pier, a small table was set up...with a white linen tablecloth, fine china and crystal glassware. A solitary candle burned brightly within the safe haven of a hurricane lamp. Standing a discreet distance away, a couple of Marines were stationed to keep other people from wandering in too close. For what he needed to say, he wanted privacy.

But he also had wanted the atmosphere of the

beach. He was hoping the memory of their walk on the sand that night they met would help his cause.

Bending slightly to one side, Harding punched a button on a nearly hidden tape recorder, and immediately the soft, delicate strains of Beethoven lifted into the cool, summer air.

He thought he saw a smile flit briefly across her face, but he couldn't be sure, because it vanished almost instantly. Then she was walking toward him, and it was all he could do to keep from going to her, drawing her close and kissing her senseless.

"What is going on, Harding?" she asked when she was within a few steps of him.

"Dinner," he said, and walked around to her side of the table. "And the chance to talk."

"You haven't been very interested in talking during the past couple of days," she said, her gaze locked on his.

It had about killed him to stay away from her. But he'd forced himself to. To give her a little time. To think. To realize that they belonged together.

Damn, why did he have to be shipping out now? Never once had being deployed bothered him. Not in the twenty years since he had signed up. Until now. Now, he couldn't bear the thought of leaving her. Of not being there to watch her body grow and swell with their child.

"Or maybe," she was saying, "you were too busy talking to everyone else to bother with talking to me directly."

He winced inwardly at her tone. All right, so he probably shouldn't have had his friends talk to her.

Obviously they hadn't accomplished what he had hoped they would.

"I'm sorry," he said softly, and reached for her unsuccessfully. She backed up, keeping a wary distance between them. "Maybe I shouldn't have, but you didn't leave me much choice, Elizabeth. I'm out of time. I had to try whatever ammunition I could come up with."

"You called my *parents!*"

"That, I'm not going to apologize for. I had to talk to your father, man to man. I'm in love with his daughter and I had to get his blessing on our marriage." That's how things were done. Couldn't she see that?

Elizabeth glared at him. "My mother called me and read me the riot act for a solid half hour because I hadn't confided in her about our 'engagement.'"

"Elizabeth—"

"I'm only surprised you didn't tell them about the—" she tossed a quick look at the two Marines, standing with their backs to them "—baby," she finished in a much quieter voice.

"I wouldn't do that without you." This was not working out as he had hoped. "Don't you get it? I *love* you."

"Stop it."

"I can't stop. And I wouldn't if I could."

She shook her head firmly. "You're only doing all of this because you're leaving. You're feeling guilty about leaving me alone and pregnant."

"You're damn right, I do!" He covered the steps separating them in two quick strides and grabbed both of her arms fiercely. "Can't you see what it's doing to me? Knowing I won't be here with you? Taking care of you?"

Her head fell back on her neck. "I told you, you don't have to worry. I'll be fine."

"But I won't." He stared into her eyes, feeling the same, swift punch to the gut he always felt when looking into their depths. "I'll be thousands of miles away from the one person I want more than my next breath."

Her features tightened, and she chewed at her bottom lip furiously. Indecision shone in her eyes, and he pressed his advantage ruthlessly.

"I want to marry you, Elizabeth. Now. Tonight. We can fly to Vegas and be back in the morning."

For one short, heart-stopping moment, he thought he had won. Then a shift of emotions clouded her eyes, and the moment was lost. Pulling away from him, she shook her head proudly.

"You can't bulldoze me into marriage, Harding."

"Elizabeth…"

"No. I won't be bullied into making such an important decision." Her heel caught in the sand, and she wobbled precariously for a minute. An ocean wind shot across the sand, lifting her hair into a wild, curly halo around her head. "You can't simply decide what's best for me and then steamroll me into agreeing with you. Marriage should be *our* decision, Harding. Not yours."

She headed for the limo. The chauffeur leaped out of the driver's seat and scurried for the back door.

Opening it just seconds before she arrived, he stood back while she slid inside.

Harding was just a step behind her. Jerking his head at the driver, he waited until the man moved off before looking down at the woman he loved and had to leave. Tears filled her eyes, but stubborn determination was stamped on her features.

Bracing both hands on the door frame, he leaned down and met her gaze squarely, silently daring her to look away. She didn't.

"Whether you believe me or not, Elizabeth. I do love you. Not just the baby. *You.*"

She didn't say a word, and he finally admitted to himself that he wasn't going to convince her. Not now. Not before he left. Pain stabbed at his heart until he thought he wouldn't be able to breathe. At last he finally understood what some of his married friends felt like when they were leaving behind all that they loved.

His fingers tightened helplessly on the cold metal. There was only one thing left to say.

"I want you to know," he said softly, "I've done what I can to protect you and the baby." He inhaled deeply, then told her, "I've named you my beneficiary and my next of kin. If anything should happen to me, you and the baby will be taken care of."

She gasped in surprise, then said, "You don't have to do that. I don't need financial help, Harding."

He scowled at her. She still didn't get it. "This isn't about money," he said firmly. "This is about honor. Love."

"I...don't know what to say." One tear spilled

from the corner of her eye and traced its way along her cheek.

"Say goodbye, Elizabeth. I leave tomorrow night."

"Tomorrow?" she said. "Already?"

He nodded. "Tell me you'll miss me. Even if it's a lie."

"Of course I'll miss you, Harding," she said as another tear traced its way down her cheek.

"Take care of yourself," he said softly.

She nodded jerkily. "You, too."

"This isn't the way I wanted to say goodbye to you, dammit," Harding growled, feeling a huge, black emptiness welling up within him. Time had run out on him. He had failed at the most important mission in his life. And now he would have to wait six long months before getting a second chance at winning her.

The months ahead stretched out in his mind, bleak and empty without her. He glanced at her trim figure and tried to imagine what she would look like, round with their child. Just the thought of all he would miss threatened to choke him. He had to go. Before he made a bigger mess than he had already.

But he couldn't leave without one last taste of her.

Bending down, he reached into the limo, cupped her face with his palms and pulled her head close. Planting his lips firmly on hers, he gave her all he had, pouring his love and concern and sorrow into a kiss that seared them both to their souls.

At last he released her and straightened away from the car. Staring down at her, he knew that this tear-streaked image of her was the one that would haunt him for six lonely months. He had had everything in the palm of his hand. How had it all disappeared so quickly?

"I love you, Elizabeth," he said, then closed the door and rapped his knuckles on the roof. The driver reacted to his signal instantly and keyed the ignition. With a muffled purr the long, white car drove away, taking Harding's world with it.

Elizabeth stared out the tinted back window until she couldn't see him anymore. Slowly she sank down into the plush seat and curled up in a corner. She'd made the right decision, she knew. A rushed marriage to a man shipping out immediately afterward wasn't the answer to a surprise pregnancy.

But if it was right...why did it suddenly feel so wrong?

Three weeks later, the first letter arrived.

Elizabeth plucked it from the stack of junk mail and tossed the circulars into the trash. Carrying the letter into the living room, she sat down in the corner of the couch and stared at the envelope in her hand. Lightly she dusted her fingertips across Harding's handwriting as if she was touching the man himself.

Lord, she missed him. More than she had imagined she would. And every day for the past three weeks, she had asked herself the same questions. Had she done the right thing in not marrying him? Or had she made the biggest mistake of her life?

Steeling herself, Elizabeth opened the envelope and slowly drew out the single sheet of paper. As slowly as a hungry man enjoying a fine meal, she devoured every word.

Dear Elizabeth,

I'm lying in my bunk wishing I was there, beside you. I know I made a mess of things before I left and I want you to know how sorry I am.

She sucked in a gulp of air and paused in her reading. Sorry? Sorry he had proposed?

You were right. I shouldn't have tried to bull-doze you into marriage. My only excuse is that I love you. And our baby. But during these weeks without you, I've realized that you need time to think about us. I want you to know I'll wait. My love won't change and it won't stop. Take care of both of you for me.

Yours, Harding

She let go of the letter, and the single page floated to her lap. Covering her mouth with one hand, she curled her legs up beneath her, laid her head on the sofa back and cried. For Harding. For herself. For lost chances.

Two months later Elizabeth reported for her first ultrasound. Her doctor had suggested the routine test as a "precaution." Uncomfortable after the seeming gallons of water she had had to drink, she stretched out on the examining table and stared at a blank TV screen.

A male technician, who looked about eighteen, with his long, pulled-back ponytail, entered the room and took a seat on the swivel stool beside her.

"All set?" he asked and readied his equipment.

"I guess so," she said, sighing.

His eyebrows rose slightly. "Well, you're the most unexcited mom I've had in here in a long time."

Mom. She shivered slightly. Even though she had broken the news to her family and everyone was now used to the idea of a baby coming, Elizabeth herself still sometimes had trouble believing it.

"So," the tech asked, "where's Dad? How come he's not here to catch the show?"

She swallowed heavily before answering. "He's overseas. In the Marines."

The teasing glint in his eyes softened a bit. "Sorry. Must be hard on him, missing all the fun."

"Yes," she muttered. "It is." She thought about the stack of letters she had received from Harding over the weeks. Almost every other day another one arrived. Lately she had found herself standing on the front porch, watching for the mailman's arrival. She tossed a glance at her purse, where all of those letters were safely tucked away. She kept them with her at all times. Somehow it made her feel closer to him. Less alone. Less afraid.

She couldn't help wondering if he felt the same about the letters she had mailed him.

"Well," the man said as he pulled back her gown and squirted cold jelly onto her abdomen, "I knew just from looking at you that you were the kind of woman whose man would be here if he could."

"You did?" She looked at him, watching him pick up the ultrasound scanner and position it above her belly.

"Sure," he said. "You see enough pregnant women, you get to know which ones are unhappy and which ones are, well, *loved*."

Tears sprung up in her eyes. Elizabeth tried to blink them back, but the salty film was too much to be denied. She swiped at the tears on her cheeks, trying to hide them from the man beside her.

"Don't worry about it," he said, and patted her hand. "In my line of work, I see crying women every day." Nodding, he assured her, "It's just the hormones."

He went about his work, smoothing the scanner up and down across her flesh, the machine making a series of soft clicking sounds as it took pictures of her womb.

Elizabeth thought about what he had said. Hormones. No, it wasn't just the changes her body was going through. It was love. And misery. The younger man had been right about Harding. He would have been here if he could. Nothing would have kept him away. She and the baby were loved. *Really* loved. How foolish of her not to have believed it before. And how stupid of her to risk losing everything because of her own fears and doubts.

"There you go," the tech said. "He-e-e-re's junior!"

Elizabeth stared at the TV screen at the tiny spot of life she and Harding had created together. Her eyes filled again even as she felt a ridiculous grin spread across her face.

"Oh, Harding," she whispered in a broken voice, "I wish you were here."

Harding pulled the grainy eight-by-ten photo out of the envelope and studied it. What the hell? In bright red ink, someone had circled a small blob of *something* in the photo. Holding the picture in one hand, he picked up Elizabeth's letter and read it, hoping for a clue.

In seconds he had dropped the letter to his bunk and was holding the photograph under the desk lamp. A slow smile curved his lips as his gaze locked on the circled blob.

His baby.

Turning around quickly, he snatched at the letter and finished reading it. As he read the last paragraph, his smile faded and a worried frown creased his features.

Harding, when you get back, I'd like for us to sit down together and talk about all of this. Surely after six months apart, we'll both be certain about what we want. And what we don't want. Take care of yourself. I miss you.

Elizabeth

Damn. What did that mean? He winced inwardly. He knew just what it meant. Hadn't he lived through this before? Hadn't his ex-wife left him while he was deployed? Why should he expect Elizabeth—who hadn't even wanted to marry him—to be waiting for him with open arms?

He glanced at his child's first picture again and felt the first stirrings of fear thread through him.

Elizabeth stood near the back of the crowd. Hundreds of wives, mothers, husbands and children were stretched out along the edge of the Camp Pendleton parade deck. Signs dotted the eager crowd. Hand-painted with more love than style, they read Ooo-rah! and Get Some! the battalion's motto. There were other, more personal signs being waved high in the air by family members counting the minutes until their loved one arrived.

Elizabeth's fingers curled over her own sign as she clutched it tightly directly in front of her rounded belly. Maybe she shouldn't have come. Maybe she should have waited for him to call her. That's what she had planned to do. But at the last minute she had decided that the best way for her to know how Harding truly felt about her was to watch his expression when he unexpectedly caught sight of her.

She only hoped she would see what she wanted to see. Smiling at the families around her, she remembered other times, other bases. She recalled clearly, running into her father's arms as he came home from duty, and the all-encompassing sense of love that would wrap around her when he picked her up and swung her in the air.

Home wasn't a building. Home was love. The love that lived within the boundaries of a family.

That's what she wanted. That sense of belonging. With Harding.

"Here they come!" someone shouted, and Elizabeth looked up in time to see the first bus from March Air Force Base drive onto the asphalt.

She took a deep breath and watched, her heart in her throat. Within fifteen or twenty minutes the troops were assembled at attention on the parade grounds. After a brief welcome-home speech, the order, "Dismissed!" was shouted and pandemonium reigned.

Jostled as people streamed past her, Elizabeth laid one hand on her swollen stomach as if to comfort her child. Then she focused her gaze on the sea of soldiers, searching for the one face she had so longed to see.

Harding stayed near the back of the crowd. He had always been the last man off the tarmac. There had never been anyone waiting for him at the end of deployment. And this time would be no different. Elizabeth had already written him that she wouldn't be there to greet him. She would be waiting at home for his call.

He stopped dead as a young private darted in front of him, beelining toward a heavily pregnant, grinning woman. Harding watched their reunion for a moment, then continued on, slower than before. Better than being trampled in the rush of men running to their wives and kids. Slowly he walked across the tarmac, trying to ignore his friends' happiness. All around him new babies were being admired, and the kisses being shared were hot enough to melt the pavement.

He closed his eyes to everything, determined not

to torture himself unnecessarily. He didn't begrudge them their moments of joy. Blast it, he would have liked to be a part of it himself.

Shifting his duffel bag to his other shoulder, he continued to weave his way through the noisy crowd. In the distance he heard the base band strike up a tune, but he wasn't really listening. He slowed his steps, deliberately putting off the time when he would have to enter his empty quarters.

An aching loneliness settled in the pit of his stomach. What if he couldn't convince Elizabeth to marry him? What if he lost her and the child he already loved? He didn't know if he would be able to stand that kind of pain.

"Hey, Hard Case," someone close by shouted and he half turned to see Staff Sergeant Jack Macguire running up to him, hand outstretched. Grabbing Harding's right hand, Jack pumped it wildly for a minute before saying, "Congratulations, you old Devil Dog! Why didn't you tell me?"

"Tell you what?" Harding asked, but his question went unanswered as Jack spun around and raced back to his wife's impatient arms. He stared after his friend and mumbled, "Now what was that all about?"

Shaking his head, Harding started walking again. As he did, the crowd drifted away until he was looking directly at a lone woman standing at the edge of the tarmac. Her hair was longer than he remembered, but the lovely features, he recognized. Elizabeth. His gaze shifted to the sign she held in front of her. It read simply, "I love you."

Harding swallowed back a sudden, rushing tide of

hope inside him. Dodging around his fellow Marines, he kept his gaze locked with hers as he made his way toward her, desperately afraid that she would disappear before he reached her side.

She was here. Waiting for him. Surely that meant something. He felt a grin blossom on his face and didn't even bother trying to hide it. As he came closer, he dropped his duffel bag to the ground and stopped just inches away from her.

"You're here," he said softly, and wished all of the people, and most especially the blasted band, away.

"I had to be here," she whispered, meeting his gaze squarely. "I love you."

Something lodged in his throat, but he spoke around it. "I love you, Elizabeth. I always have."

"I know that now," she told him. "I can see it in your eyes. That's why I had to come."

He sucked in a gulp of air and risked everything he had ever wanted on one question. "Will you marry me?"

"Yes," she said quickly, tears spilling from her eyes and coursing unchecked down her cheeks.

"Ooo-rah!" Harding shouted and laughed all at once, feeling months of worry and fear fall from his shoulders like an unwanted blanket. He reached for her, but Elizabeth was still clutching that sign of hers and showed no intention of letting it drop. "Honey," he said with a smile, "to get the kind of kiss we both need, you're gonna have to let go of that so we can move in close."

Grimacing slightly, she lowered the posterboard to

reveal a very pregnant body. "I'm afraid *close* is a relative term, Harding."

Stunned, he stared at the mound of their child for a long minute before gently laying his palm atop it. She covered his hand with one of hers. The baby gave a solid kick, and Harding's eyes widened in disbelief. Finally, after too many years alone, he at last knew what it was to have a family.

"I'm fat," she whined with a half smile.

"Uh-uh, lady," he whispered as he bent to claim her lips, "you're gorgeous."

He tasted her tears and swallowed them, knowing them as the blessing they were. Love rose up around them as surely as the mounting applause from the surrounding soldiers and their families. Harding didn't care who was watching. Everything he had ever wanted was right there, held tight to his heart.

And he would never let them go.

Epilogue

Three months later.

"Ah, sweetheart," Harding whispered as he brushed her damp hair back off her forehead. "I swear to you, I'm going in for a vasectomy today."

Despite the pain, Elizabeth laughed and held his hand tightly. "Don't you dare," she told him. "I don't want junior to be an only child."

Eyes wild, he bent, kissed her forehead, then looked at her like she was crazy. "How can you even *think* about another baby now?"

The crushing pain ebbed slightly, and she lifted her gaze to her harried husband's worried features. God, how she loved him. Every day she gave thanks for whatever fates had brought them together.

"Don't worry so much, Harding," she said, then gasped as the next pain rushed at her, "I'm not the first woman to have a baby."

Whatever he might have said was lost as the doctor announced, "All right, everybody, it's showtime! Harding, get behind your wife and prop her up."

As he moved to follow orders, Harding brushed a kiss on the top of her head and whispered, "I love you."

"Me, too," she said, concentrating entirely on the task at hand.

"Here we go, Elizabeth, bear down."

She did and in minutes, her son had entered the world, screaming his displeasure. Breathing deeply, Elizabeth lay back down and watched the doctor lift her baby so that she could get a good look at him before handing the newborn to his father.

Harding held the squirming infant confidently, as he did everything in his life. She smiled gently as she watched her bear of a Marine tenderly inspect his child with a loving touch and a soothing whisper of sound. At last he looked at her, his blue eyes brimming with unshed tears, his face touched with a smile of wonder.

"He's beautiful, Elizabeth," he said, and gently laid their son in the crook of his mother's arm. Bending protectively over them, he planted a quick, gentle kiss at the corner of her mouth. "Thank you," he said in a tone meant only for her to hear. "Thank you for bringing me to life."

She reached up and caressed his cheek, wiping away a stray tear with her fingertips. Smiling up at

him, she said, "I love you, Harding." Then she
winked and promised, "And don't worry. I won't tell
your little Marine friends that their 'Hard Case'
should really be called 'Soft Touch.'"

* * * * *

Look for Maureen Child's next book,
THE NON-COMMISSIONED BABY,
book two of
THE BACHELOR BATTALION series,
coming in October,
only from Silhouette Desire.

SILHOUETTE® *Desire*®

THE RULE BREAKERS

an exciting new series by
Leanne Banks

Meet The Rulebreakers: A millionaire, a bad boy, a protector. Three strong, sexy men who take on the ultimate challenge—love!

Coming in September 1998—MILLIONAIRE DAD

Joe Caruthers had it all. Who would have thought that a brainy beauty like Marley Fuller—pregnant with his child—would cause this bachelor with everything to take the plunge?

Coming in October 1998—
THE LONE RIDER TAKES A BRIDE

Bad boy Ben Palmer had rebelled against falling in love, until he took the lovely, sad-eyed Amelia Russell on a moonlit ride.

Coming in November 1998—THIRTY-DAY FIANCÉ

Nick Nolan had to pretend to be engaged to his childhood friend Olivia Polnecek. Why was Nick noticing how perfect a wife she could be—for real!

Available at your favorite retail outlet.

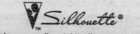

Silhouette®

SDRULE

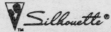

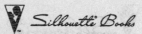

INTIMATE MOMENTS®
Silhouette®

**Coming in October from
Silhouette Intimate Moments...**

BRIDES OF THE NIGHT

Silhouette Intimate Moments fulfills your wildest
wishes in this compelling new in-line collection
featuring two very memorable men...tantalizing,
irresistible men who exist only in the darkness
but who hunger for the light of true love.

TWILIGHT VOWS
by Maggie Shayne

The unforgettable WINGS IN THE NIGHT miniseries
continues with a vampire hero to die for and the
lovely mortal woman who will go to any lengths to
save their unexpected love.

MARRIED BY DAWN
by Marilyn Tracy

Twelve hours was all the time this rogue vampire
had to protect an innocent woman. But was
marriage his only choice to keep her safe—if not
from the night...then from himself?

*Look for BRIDES OF THE NIGHT this October,
wherever Silhouette books are sold.*

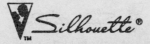

Silhouette®

Look us up on-line at: http://www.romance.net   SIMBON

MATERNITY LEAVE

Coming September 1998

Three delightful stories about the blessings
and surprises of "Labor" Day.

TABLOID BABY by Candace Camp

She was whisked to the hospital in the nick of time....

THE NINE-MONTH KNIGHT
by Cait London

A down-on-her-luck secretary is experiencing
odd little midnight cravings....

THE PATERNITY TEST by Sherryl Woods

The stick turned blue before her
biological clock struck twelve....

*These three special women are very pregnant...and very
single, although they won't be either for too much longer,
because baby—and Daddy—are on their way!*

Available at your favorite retail outlet.

SILHOUETTE® Desire®

COMING NEXT MONTH